Nancy

Maybe this Book will
change how you do
things! Mitch

The Fishy Side of Real Estate

A Novel by Mitch Vogel

Mitch Vogel

Clear Choice Realtors

Indianapolis, IN

www.ccrealtors.net

Editing and proofreading:

Claudia Grossmann

Lisa Taylor

Book and cover design:

Sara Love

ISBN 978-0-578-10109-5

Most of this book is true.

I want to thank all the people – my clients and the people working in our local real estate market – who helped to inspire me to address an issue nobody else wanted to talk about.

Find out more about the ethical concept at: www.ccrealtors.net.

PART ONE

"It's all I can
stands and I can't
stands no more!"

-Popeye

The 30 Second Rule

January 16, 2011

On a clear winter day, three men sat for a business lunch at the Skyline Club atop one of the tallest buildings in downtown Indianapolis, Indiana. The view sprawled in all directions, a spectacular one. Planes descended silently past the window, as the landing pattern passed over the north edge of the downtown area. The snow patches below magnified the brightness of the day. It was ten degrees outside.

Two of the men were attorneys. Both were independents working for their own small firms. The other was an independent real estate broker. They all shared the same disdain for large companies that focus on profit rather than the job at hand. They had that bond in common – small time mavericks working hard for their money.

They were friends and cohorts meeting on an irregular basis.

Vance Ingalls, a local patent attorney, leaned over his plate and stuffed the remaining Caesar salad into his mouth.

Miles Vincent, the independent broker who had branched out on his own from a large local real estate company, had introduced a new real estate concept that was raising eyebrows. His start-up real estate company was called Clear Choice Realtors. He had introduced the idea three years ago and although he had gotten positive responses from his clients, the idea was slow to catch on with the general public.

"Look Miles, I'm telling you that you only have 30 seconds to get their attention, otherwise, your idea will never work," Vance stated.

Miles replied ruefully, "Yeah, I understand. But I cannot explain the idea in 30 seconds!"

He was obviously flustered by the lack of response to his company's new business model.

Jake Brandon, an independent patent attorney who was known for his charming wit and stodgy attire, broke in – "Vance is right, Miles. Consumers would find your concept appealing, but since the idea is so different, you would have to launch a large educational campaign to get the concept across."

"Are consumers really that slow?" asked Miles, with his usual look of disbelief wracked across his face. "You guys know why I'm doing this."

Miles had complained about it before, but he was baffled by the responses from various colleagues in his own line of work. Over the past couple of years, Miles had reached out to people whom he thought would embrace a business concept that would improve the relationship formed between the agent and the client. He had reached out to members of the local real estate board, mortgage companies, other brokers and others who made the ship of real estate sail. Even though Miles had improved the business model, those in the real estate industry were not ready for this kind of change.

Vance rested back in his chair and rolled his eyes, thinking of a meeting he had later on with an important client. He hoped Miles wasn't about to jump on his preaching wagon.

In the next instant, Miles replied, "But I am not getting into what you both already know."

Both attorneys had heard the argument before. No one disagreed with Miles' point, but changing the status quo – to change the public perception on established real estate business practices, is a pursuit against the current, like swimming upstream. Miles had made up his mind to improve the fundamental relationships that are established between the agent and the client. The best way to exemplify that improvement is to practice it. He had been doing that in a manner that many would consider 'under the radar'.

Most agents who worked in real estate understood the inherent conflict of interest that accompanied limited agency, also known as dual agency, which can happen when one real estate agent represents both the buyer and the seller in the same transaction. Miles' new business concept eliminated that situation. When he first started the business, he thought his idea would be embraced by those who worked alongside him in the real estate business. But they didn't.

Even the local papers refused to provide any coverage of the new concept.

"Stop being so sappy about your situation and concentrate on the people who will most value the service," Vance said, "but I'm telling you Miles, you got thirty seconds to get your point across or it won't fly."

Jake glanced at his phone. They all had places to go.

○

○

○

Open House

May 20, 2007

Miles Vincent was having the time of his life. He worked for the number one broker in the city of Indianapolis, Trinity Real Estate. He was in the top five percent in sales production for the entire metro area. 2007 was a banner year for realtors. All across the country real estate firms were getting rich, along with everyone else in the mortgage and finance industry. Nearly every deal made the closing table.

Money was flowing. Deals were flying. Lenders approved everything. Real estate seminars were packed. Anyone could get financing with little or no money down. Although it seemed like a joke, it wasn't.

But it was during this gold rush that Miles Vincent would experience something that would change the way he thought about real estate, at least from a client service perspective.

On this particular day, at an open house where everything was ready, the stage was set for another day of home showing. The sign at the corner of Buckle Street and Vine Avenue said, *'Open House 12-3, 901 Buckle St. Trinity Real Estate, Miles Vincent, Realtor.'*

Melanie and Andrew Berlin had been married one year. This was Drew's fourth year at Simon Properties, a large commercial real estate firm that had its headquarters directly across from the Indiana Statehouse. It was Melanie's second year working at the downtown Nordstrom. They met at the mall two years ago. Now the couple wanted to buy a house and had planned to visit open houses in the downtown area. The older homes attracted them. They both liked the high ceilings, wooden floors and the warmth that comes with a vintage-style home. They had both grown up in older homes and preferred the diversity of the inner city as opposed to the more affluent outlying areas. They liked the fringe.

Melanie's Honda pulled in front of the house. Heavy rain drops began to splat around them. Drew yelled, "Mel, hurry up, I think it's going to pour!" The drops multiplied in seconds as they scurried up the sidewalk, thick popping sounds filling the air. They reached the porch as the crack of thunder exploded above them.

"Wow, was that close!" They had said the words together, at the exact same moment. They hugged each other on the porch as the skies opened up. It was a downpour. A gust of wind made the porch swing sway and creak. The couple turned toward the front door. The sign on it said, 'Come in!'

Andrew opened the door. They went inside.

The stunning entryway caught their breath as they entered the parlor of a show-fit, historic home, tastefully restored in every detail. Every light in the house was on. The floors were sparkling oak, the chandelier glistened, but the grand staircase was the centerpiece. Thunder was grumbling in the background.

"Oh my God, Drew! It's better than the photos! And it's in our price range."

Drew walked over to the staircase placing his hand on the finial. "Nice."

They heard steps approaching from the back as a sharp-dressed Miles Vincent approached from the kitchen. "Good afternoon! You just made it in before the downpour!" Miles stretched out his hand to Drew. "Hi, I'm Miles Vincent from Trinity Real Estate, the listing agent," he said simply. Simplicity, Miles always remembered, was the best way to start.

They shook hands. Miles turned to Melanie, "Pleased to meet you." He nodded to Melanie.

"My name is Melanie. Nice to meet you, Miles," she said.

As a top producer, Miles had completed hundreds of transactions during his 12 years in the business. From these experiences, he had honed an intuition about reading potential clients. What they said, how they said it, the body language someone uses: he could already tell the couple was interested in the home before they said anything.

Suddenly, the rain slowed down making things quieter. They all looked outside. "Isn't this a great neighborhood?" Miles questioned, but it was more of a statement. "You can tell that many homes have been improved in this historic area, but this home has much of its original detail still intact."

Andrew and Melanie were staring at the staircase. Then, as they were standing at the base of the stairs, the sky gave way to a patch of blue which beamed sunlight directly on and into the house. The effect was magical. The sun had illuminated the 901 Buckle home to its best. It was so bright that the inside lights could have been off, for even the brightest light in the house was dull against the sun's radiance. The original leaded glass window atop the stair landing refracted the sunlight, casting rainbow prisms everywhere. It was movie-like.

Melanie and Andrew started up the newly lit grand staircase.

"Are you folks in the market for buying a home?" Miles didn't waste any time getting down to business as he followed them up the grand staircase.

The Listing

May 13, 2007

Miles Vincent was a listing machine. He had a natural ability to discover common ground between himself and someone he had never met before. Such was the case at a new listing opportunity at 901 Buckle Street.

Buckle Street was in the heart of the city's historic district. Older homes, many that had fallen into disrepair over years of neglect, were being fixed up. The neighborhood was making a comeback and real estate sales were strong. Miles was an expert in this neighborhood. He knew the history. He knew which famous families had built particular homes. He could explain the differences between the styles of homes. Whether the home was a Queen Anne, Victorian, American Four Square, or Craftsman Bungalow; Miles would point out specific details illustrating each. He knew his architecture.

Miles walked up the sidewalk to 901 Buckle. It was a classic 3-story Colonial Revival. Miles could give a lecture on the homes built during the late 1890s until the early 1920s. He stood there for a moment to collect his thoughts before going inside to meet the seller, Marty Miller.

Miller had bought the home only three years ago, but had done a lot of improvements. He had tried to sell the house on his own, but selling a house is not as easy as it sounds. So he called a realtor. He had called Miles.

Miles rapped three times with the antique knocker. Within moments the door swung open revealing the owner.

"Hello. You must be Miles. Please come in," the man in the doorway said.

Miles walked into the parlor, admiring the finishes. "Your house looks beautiful, Mr. Miller. And what a grand staircase to show it off!" remarked Miles as he made a sweeping gesture with his arm, but not too fast, demonstrating his artistic aplomb.

"Please, come into the kitchen where we can talk business," Miller said, motioning toward the back of the house. The floors were newly sealed but still made squeaking sounds as they passed through the dining room. Miles noticed the original pocket doors still in place. He was admiring the details of the home.

The kitchen was bright and orderly. Marty headed for the kitchen table where he did most of his work. Stacks of paper, some file folders, various condiments and other things messed up an otherwise tidy kitchen.

Marty offered Miles a seat on the least messy side of the table. "Well, Mr. Vincent, let's see what you have for me."

Miles began his well rehearsed spiel. He covered the company's dynamic marketing plan, the hybrid use of the internet, the exposure and statistics, which were true and convincing. Miles demonstrated his personal success alongside the numbers posted by Trinity Real Estate; impressive statistics to say the least. Marty liked what he saw.

Miles saved the most important issues for last: the market analysis and net sheet. The market analysis was a comparison of other similar properties in the area that had sold recently. A realtor takes the aggregate average of those comparables and comes up with a value for a particular property. Not exactly rocket science, but very effective for determining market value of a given residential property. The net sheet shows how much the seller takes home after all expenses have been estimated and subtracted from market value. That number is what most sellers are interested in – the net proceeds of the sale. Just how important is the profit realized from the sale of someone's home? If the real estate agent can come close to the estimated sale price then the net proceeds are pretty easy to determine.

Miles got to the page of his listing presentation where those comparables were represented by numbers. Marty quickly eyeballed the number at the bottom of the page: it was the proposed listing price. His eyes got bigger and his heart raced. Then Marty blurted out, "Miles, that number is too low!" and jabbed his finger at the number representing the estimated value of his home. "Two-ninety-nine is not going to cut it!"

Miles looked at Marty, whose face was screwed on with certain finality, as though his arms should have been crossed. "Mr. Miller, with all due respect, I have been more than generous with my calculations, and I feel this listing price is accurate based on the area comparables," replied Miles stoically.

Marty leaned back and folded his arms. "If you list my home for three twenty-five, you got the contract," he said flatly. "And I'll sign the papers right now."

This moment was always the crux of the situation. This was the moment all listing agents covet: the contract signature. The contract signature ensured a relationship and an obligation, and the listing contract was the hammered-out doctrine that allowed real estate brokers to collect. And collecting the green stuff ranks pretty high on the priority list for almost everyone.

Miles knew his agency obligations like the back of his hand. Those attributes that defined the relationship between the client and himself, the agent, and the duty owed to the client. He took his agency obligations seriously. Seared into his brain were the hallowed attributes owed to the client:

'Care. Acccountability. Loyalty. Obedience. Disclosure.'

Those attributes were always swimming around in Miles' head. He knew the muddy waters of real estate and worked hard to earn his money. He also did it in a way that followed the code, and he always let the code guide his decisions and actions.

"Obey the client", Miles thought to himself, respecting the code.

Smiling broadly, Miles extended his hand across the table. "Three twenty-five it is! And we have a deal!" said Miles. The two shook hands.

Miles reached to pull out a stack of various forms that accompany a listing contract. There is no reason to delay once the client makes his decision, Miles reminded himself.

"There are a few documents to sign, Mr. Miller."

"Think you can have an open house next Sunday, Miles?" Marty asked.

"I'll be happy to do it," Miles replied.

And he didn't even do the net sheet, the calculation that showed the seller, to within a thousand or two, the net amount of money he would be taking to the bank. The listing contract was already in his hand. Miles spent the next hour explaining the contract, getting all the proper signatures, including agency disclosure, which was always neatly contained within the listing contract. Miles pointed out that a formal agency relationship between the two of them began as soon as the seller signed the contract. Miles was careful to outline his agency responsibility to his new client. He discussed that the possibility of limited agency (when the agent represents both the seller and buyer) could arise. In fact, it said so right in the listing contract. In the excitement of the contract, not much attention is paid to that disclosure by the client.

The Offer

May 20, 2007

Melanie and Drew had been in the house at 901 Buckle for nearly an hour. A few other people had come and gone, but the couple didn't seem to notice. The house had bitten them. They were infected with its charm. They were placing particular pieces of furniture in certain rooms.

Miles knew they were interested. He gave them their space, yet was there – almost instantaneously – if needed. Indeed, he mused to himself, it really was like deep sea fishing – the time, the patience, the preparation. Then the journey begins, like a captain who prepares his fishing boat the day before the expedition, and now he is steering the boat out to sea toward the targeted fishing destination. The lines drop in, the silvery ribbon fish at the end of a 40lb test line, flashing and whipping, a tempting appetizer for a big fish. 'No ocean in Indiana', he reminded himself, 'you cannot make a fish take bait; patience is required while deep sea fishing.'

Back in his college days, Miles worked as a deck hand on fishing charters running out of Port Aransas, Texas. Port Aransas had a small harbor, mostly dedicated to sport fishing. It was those carefree fishing days on the Gulf that hooked Miles – he loved the ocean. His mind would often drift back to those lazy summer days and the hours of idling in the blue Gulf of Mexico: the heat, the humidity, the boredom of fishing, the quiet rocking at sea, the smell of diesel fumes. Then the riveting change of awareness when the fishing reel begins to click, slow at first, then bait is taken, and everyone is transfixed on the fish at the end of the line, the reel spinning and screaming. Miles imagined all those incredible sport fishing days. He had seen his share of trophy fish hauled in: blue marlin, sailfish, ling cod, snapper, red drum. He even liked catching kingfish because the locals had shown him how to clean them so the meat wouldn't turn dark. And kingfish put up a really good fight.

He was lost in kingfish thought when Melanie approached him with Drew in tow.

"Miles," she said as she grabbed Andrew's hand, "we want to make an offer on this property."

The fish had just bit hard on the bait.

It was all business now. Miles washed the brackish images of the Texas Gulf from his memory. "That's great!" replied Miles. "Let's go back to the kitchen and talk about what we need to do."

There was a sense of urgency now. The lightness in his step whisked them toward the kitchen, to the same table where Miles had signed the listing contract with Marty Miller just one week ago. Now the table was clean with a small vase of flowers on it. All of Marty's mess had been moved, not that the mess had been eliminated, but just relocated to a less public area. Actually, Marty had stuffed the entire contents into a cardboard box and put it under the sink.

Miles knew that this was a time for action. He knew all the rules. He had all the proper forms with him. Miles had perfected the art of real estate etiquette. During the entire process, he rarely made mistakes. Miles took his real estate seriously. After all, things were really serious now that Miles was about to double his projected commission if he represented both sides of the transaction: the buyer and the seller. He didn't like to think about it.

In real estate lingo, that's called a 'me and me'. Me gets paid twice. It didn't take Miles long to figure that his $11,375 cut would double to $22,750. The other side of the commission was the easy money. Miles felt an unwanted cringe creep across his forehead. And it wasn't because of the easy money. Or was it?

He had done it before: represented the buyer and seller in the same deal.

Miles actually didn't like doing it, but his composure was resolute in dealing with a transaction where he represented both buyer and seller. Miles believed deep inside him that it was wrong. The training he received from Trinity was exemplary but even upper management dismissed the vagaries of dual agency; the situation whereby the agent could end up compromising his ability when representing both the buyer and seller simultaneously.

But he knew *how* to do it.

Miles had a sudden image of a 120lb sailfish exploding out of sapphire colored water, fringed in white foam.

They entered the kitchen and went to the table. All three sat up straight. A moment of silence put everything into perspective.

Miles began. "Drew, Melanie," he looked directly at each client when he said their names. "This can sometimes happen like this…that people find something they want and just go for it. As you know, I am the listing agent for this house, so I represent the seller. But the State of Indiana allows us to represent both the buyer and seller. So, if you feel comfortable with that, we could go right into drafting a purchase agreement. The State requires an additional document that states that both the buyer and seller agree to allow the agent to represent both. The document describes our agency limitations, and I must explain it all to you. I won't be able to give any contractual advantage to either client – the buyer or the seller. How do you feel about that?" Miles asked.

Melanie reached under the table to hold Drew's hand, disregarding the importance of Miles' disclosure and said, "We have been looking for a while and we know this is the house we want to buy. We both feel comfortable," she turned to look at Drew, "and we just know that this is the place. It is *so* us. We think you are honest and we think we want to proceed. We have done our homework, too." Melanie reached into her purse and pulled out an envelope. "We have already been pre-approved for the mortgage! We just needed to find the house!" she stated happily.

Miles opened the letter. It was a pre-approval letter from a local mortgage broker. They were approved for a loan up to $415,000. Miles smiled inwardly. Normally, pre-approving buyers is part of the process, but much to his benefit, the Berlins had been proactive in getting their financial act together.

"So you are both ok with me representing you as your agent?" Miles asked. "We want this house before someone else gets it," said Drew.

Miles reached over to a folder and placed it on the table. He took out a stack of forms related to the purchase of a home.

Again, the internal mantra went off in Miles' brain before he spoke. 'Client obligations: care – accountability – loyalty – obedience – and disclosure.' He always went according to the rules and procedures, every step of the way. In fact, Miles was an ace in continuing education. Every two years, realtors are expected to take 16 course hours of continuing education for real estate. Every two years, an agent must take the identical courses and take the same, identical tests to ensure they remain sharp in the field. He prided himself in doing well and always aced the quizzes when it came time for the testing.

Now he was putting all that good training to use.

Miles was kind of an odd-ball when it came to business ethics. He stuck to the rules based on his understanding of how the real estate Code of Ethics should be applied in the workplace. The real estate Code of Ethics was written vaguely, so it encouraged a variety of perspectives. The vagueness of the text actually protected real estate agents because the rules had a serious lack of objective definition – if there's no real clarity in the definition, then it's hard for anyone to pinpoint misdeeds in the workplace. Licensed real estate agents are required to take continuing education classes every two years and Miles actually looked forward to taking the classes. He was especially interested in the Code of Ethics. His understanding of agency law could answer many questions correctly on the LSAT.

Miles arranged the documents: the purchase agreement, the seller's disclosure statement, the lead-based paint disclosure, the Trinity Real Estate agency disclosure statement, and one more, the Limited Agency Disclosure Form, which was required by the State of Indiana for transactions whereby the agent is representing both the buyer and seller.

He knew all of these documents well. It seemed like a lot of paperwork, and it was. But certain forms were necessary – for everyone's protection.

Miles began with the purchase agreement. He started by asking Melanie and Andrew the correct legal spelling of their names. Miles was careful and slow when he explained the purchase agreement – it was the driving document for a legal property transaction.

Then they approached the line for how much the couple would offer for the home. Miles knew he had to be careful. "Yes, here we are to the purchase price," Miles said, but inside he felt a little uncomfortable. He knew the rules of dual agency and the Indiana State disclosure form stated the following: the agent can only state the current purchase price and nothing less! He also must disclose to his new clients that the State disclosure specifically states that the limited agent (Miles) cannot give either buyer or seller a contractual advantage during the course of the transaction. Such limitations! The agent's ability to give 100% to the buyers has evaporated, like the air siphoned out of a room so that there is nothing to breathe. Real estate agents merely hold their breath until it's over.

Miles thought back to the week before when he was at the exact same table sitting with Marty Miller. He had shown him the comparative analysis work, and yet when Marty blurted out his own price, he had to deal with the pressure of the moment, the need to appease the client and achieve a monetary goal that, according to Trinity, was at the top of the priority list.

And now Miles was on the brink of another deal.

"In this market, I would suggest making a full price offer at $325,000." He was in line with the rules – *that the limited agent cannot say that the seller will accept anything less than the listed price*. Yes, Miles remembered, that was *exactly* the rule.

After all, they were approved for $415,000. Like a shot of tequila, the pre-approved amount lessened the guilt for Miles.

Then Andrew spoke. "Let's make it a full price offer."

There, it was done. The worst of the worrying was over. Using his 10-carat, gold-filled Trinity Top Producer ink pen, he wrote in the amount that would make his seller the happiest: $325,000.

Miles breezed through the rest of the documents, got the proper signatures and explained what was required. After an hour, Miles had arranged all the signed documentation, gotten the signed earnest money deposit and had the originals neatly placed in front of him. Miles said, "This is really exciting for all of us! I'll need to get copies of everything for you soon. But I will get this offer presented to the seller today. My feeling is that this strong offer will stand a very good chance of being accepted!"

And Miles was right.

But Miles also felt a pang of remorse. He struggled with his compromised role because he had done less than his best job – but the Berlins were happy.

He believed the seller would be thrilled with a full-price offer. The remorse came from the feeling about what he believed the house was worth and what the buyers were offering to pay. Had he done them an injustice? Was his best service as an agent held hostage by the predicament of limited agency? 'As long as the disclosure is signed,' Miles thought to himself, 'everything will be fine.'

They stood up from the kitchen table. Melanie hugged Miles. Miles shook Drew's hand. They all headed toward the door. "I am soooo excited!" Melanie squealed.

They stopped at the staircase a moment. "It's going to be ours," said Drew as he put his arm around Melanie's waist. Miles escorted them out the door and onto the porch.

"I'll be in touch soon!" said Miles. The happy couple waved goodbye as they walked to the car. Miles turned and removed the 'Come In!' sign hanging on the door. The open house was over.

Miles went inside, closed the door and called the seller to tell him the good news about the open house. Marty was ecstatic about the full price offer. Without any hesitation, he accepted the offer.

When Miles got home Sunday evening, he had completed the deal, gotten the signatures, and was already thinking about Monday as he finally got to read the Sunday paper. There were other deals he had to work on.

Asking for Help

May 21, 2007

Miles sat in his car at a stoplight. He was headed to the Trinity office to turn in paperwork, check the activity over the weekend. It was Monday morning – time to talk in the office with the other agents about the local market and whatnot.

Miles was still mulling over yesterday's event. He had decided that he would have a talk with the office manager, Terry Hanover. There was something eating away at him and he needed to talk. Mondays were perfect for that – a time for all agents to discuss their ideas, their challenges, their stories.

Miles pulled into the lot at 8:30 am sharp. He was the first agent there although the office secretaries got there at eight. Miles noticed that Terry's car was in its customary spot. Miles knew it was the perfect time to discuss his thoughts. He pulled in, grabbed some file folders off the seat and headed into the Trinity office.

Miles went in the front door of Trinity Real Estate. The company had a number of offices around the city. The north side Trinity office had a reputation for developing top producers. Miles was one of them.

Miles passed by Terry's office door, which was open and he saw Terry going over some paperwork. He stuck his head in the door. "Morning, Terry. Got a few minutes to talk this morning?"

Terry looked up. "Morning, Miles. Sure, give me a couple minutes to get this report done."

"Ok," replied Miles and headed back to his office. Fleetwood Mac was playing overhead. Miles remembered seeing them in Austin. It was the 1975 tour and Stevie Nicks had joined the band. Miles envisioned the last time he saw Stevie Nicks on TV. She wasn't the same twenty-something he saw in 1975. Of course, neither was he.

Miles turned the light on and went to his desk. He sat down and placed the file folders on his desk. He leaned over to the flat, lateral file and opened it to see dozens of suspended hanging files that held his work: listing files, pending contracts, closed contracts, company information, local, state and national files, information for buyers, sellers, and a section for continuing education. It was like a large tackle box of paperwork.

Miles sorted the stack and began putting them in the file cabinet. He came to the listing file for Marty Miller, the listing contract he had just signed eight days ago. Now it was going into the pending transaction file. Miles looked at the next file. It contained the paperwork for the Berlins' offer on Buckle St. He stared at it for a moment, then got up and walked over to Terry's office.

Miles rapped on the open door. "You finished yet, Terry?"

Terry looked up and said, "Sure am, Miles, c'mon in."

Miles walked in and sat on one of the two chairs positioned in front of Terry's desk.

"What's on your mind?" asked Terry. Miles sat in the chair, leaned back and stretched out his legs.

"Well," began Miles, "something is bugging me." Miles explained the Buckle Street dilemma. He recited the agency attributes owed to each client during a transaction, especially in the case of representing the seller, Marty Miller, and then the subsequent representation of the Berlins as the buyers. Miles felt that he had done an injustice because he could not represent the buyers to the best of his ability. In the end, he felt that they overpaid for the home, and that bothered him greatly. He had compromised his ability to help his buyers get the best price possible.

"But you followed the process exactly to the letter of the law, Miles," Terry explained while he tapped a pen on the desk. "There's no shame in that. You have done everything correctly, just like you always do."

"Yeah, maybe I followed the rules, but I feel like there has been a huge injustice done on my part," Miles said, his voice complaining, like a fly in the room.

"Miles, Miles, Miles," Terry said slowly, "you made the disclosures and got the proper signatures. What else do you need to do?"

Miles paused for a moment, knowing that Terry was not sympathetic to the ethical dilemma that bothered him. "I don't know. I'm talking about how I feel, that's all."

Terry grabbed a sheet from a stack of papers .on his desk. "Miles, look at your production this year, and we're not even to the end of the second quarter," as he held the paper up and pointed to a line that represented Miles' production. "Look at that, you have closed seven million dollars already!"

Terry was a statistics freak. He was all about the numbers. Trinity was all about numbers. "Miles, my man," Terry said somewhat affectionately, "you have got to lighten up on this. You are making $20,000 on the Buckle deal and you look like you just killed the family hamster."

"You're right, Terry," Miles stated, though he thought the Berlins were better than hamsters. He stood up and reached over to shake his manager's hand, "Thanks for talking to me this morning."

"Anytime, Miles!" Terry said loudly, a sound that concluded the meeting.

Miles left knowing that his discussion with Terry did nothing to deal with the ethics issue that was still swimming in his head.

But Miles had other fish to fry.

A Family Call

May 29, 2007

Miles was at his desk a few minutes before 8 am when his cell phone rang. He picked it up and looked at the incoming call. It was from his uncle Joe who lived in Montezuma, a small river town on the Wabash River, north of Terre Haute.

Miles answered immediately, "Hello Uncle Joe! What a nice surprise to hear from you. How's retirement these days?"

"Oh, it's ok, but not that great. Sorry to bother you Miles, because I know you're busy selling houses."

"You're not bothering me at all," Miles interrupted, "you can call me anytime you want."

"That's awfully nice of you, Miles. The reason for my call is that I want to sell the house here in Montezuma – you know that I have wanted to move to Florida for a long time – and now that your Aunt Betsy has died, well, I have decided to move, Miles. And when I made that decision I knew of no one better to talk to about selling this house than my favorite nephew!"

Miles was flattered, but he knew that Montezuma was way out of his area of expertise, in fact, it would be more of a disservice to his uncle to list his home, but relatives never seemed to understand that, they just see your stats and think you can sell anything, anywhere, at any time.

"Uncle Joe – thanks for thinking of me, but you know Montezuma is a long way from Indy and it might make more sense for you to use somebody local."

"But Miles, I don't want anybody else to list the house!" Uncle Joe complained.

Miles replied, "But I don't know the area that well."

"Yes you do, you spent your summers out here," stated Uncle Joe.

Then over the office loudspeaker system was the announcement for the weekly sales meeting. They always began promptly at 8 am on Tuesdays.

"Uncle Joe, I am sorry, but our sales meeting is beginning soon. Can I give you a call back?" asked Miles.

"Sure Miles, I know you're busy. Call me when you can," replied Uncle Joe.

"Will do Uncle Joe, talk to you later."

"Goodbye Miles."

Miles cleared off his desk as he got ready for the sales meeting. First he needed some coffee. As he headed over to the coffee machine, where other agents had gathered prior to the meeting to do the same thing, Miles thought about his summers in Montezuma and specifically about the time when he was about nine years old and he had seen something that he had never forgotten – a huge catfish when he was with Uncle Joe hiking along the Wabash River. They had walked up on an old black man and a boy, maybe his grandson, and the two had pulled in a huge catfish out of the water. Miles was scared of the huge monster with its twitching whiskers. It glistened with slime and lay on the ground, writhing. It was Miles' first experience with a big fish.

"Coffee, Miles?" asked Kat Thrasher, a hot, top-producer who worked the north side, the more affluent suburbs. She wore purple nail polish. A tiny champagne-colored tourmaline adorned her left pinky fingernail.

"Oh, sure," said Miles thinking about the catfish, then suddenly noticing the sparkle on Kat's left hand.

Kat noticed he was spacey and asked, "You all right, Miles?"

"Hi Kat, yes, well I was lost in thought, you know. Coffee sounds great. Looks like everyone's headed in for the meeting," Miles said, but he was thinking about his Uncle Joe in Montezuma and that catfish as Kat extended a coffee, her left pinky fingernail flashing like a fishing lure, taunting Miles.

Into the sales meeting they went.

Help on the Way

May 31 2007

Miles was in his car at 7:30 am headed to the office. The Thursday morning was cool, but he had the windows down as he drove his spotless BMW 320i north on College Avenue. Most of the traffic was headed in the opposite direction, toward downtown. Miles was lucky he was driving against the flow. NPR was on the radio; Miles liked the BBC morning news.

Miles was thinking about calling his Uncle Joe when he got into the office. He didn't pay attention to the radio, but rather, he thought about what he could do to help his Uncle Joe. Maybe he could refer the listing instead. Referrals are common practice in the real estate industry and an agent can make extra money by referring business to other agents.

There is a lot of money to be made in referral; in fact, some larger companies will have departments within HR that deal with the moving and relocating of employees. These relocation department employees negotiate a cut of the real estate commission from the sale of an employee's home. Company relocation departments solicit listing brokers for the opportunity to list the home. This is very similar to chumming: you cut up pieces of rotten fish and wait around for the biggest shark to swim by. The amount of the referral is usually the determining factor in the selection of the listing broker. It is all about money, and not much else. It is certainly not about finding the employee the most capable agent to list the home.

Generally, there is not much work in an individual referral. Miles could simply throw a dart at the realtor dartboard in west-central Indiana and score a 20% cut of the listing side commission. One phone call and that's it. Weeks later the referring realtor gets a check. Not a bad way to make some extra cash.

But Miles wanted to help his uncle. As he pulled onto Meridian Street a few blocks from the Trinity office, his creative wheels spun like a one-armed bandit.

"I've got it," and his eyes widened with excitement. He was so excited he pulled into the parking lot more quickly, even squeaking the tires at the abrupt stop. He skipped to the door.

"Hi Sandy," Miles said to the office secretary as he whisked down the hallway to his office. He went in, flipped on the lights, closed the door and turned on his computer.

Miles clicked on his browser to get online, then opened the connection to RealServe, the on-line program exclusively for realtors. RealServe was the software program that all agents and brokers used for researching real estate. It was the mother lode of real estate information, containing data on all properties that had sold, pended, expired or been withdrawn, not to mention everything that was current on the market. It could link property tax information, maps and statistics; it offered agents a platform designed to create customized searches for buyers. Most agents use it as a searching tool for properties for their buyers. For sellers, it was the most important place to have their property listed, and you could only get on RealServe if you were under contract with a licensed broker.

Miles used RealServe religiously and now he thought he could use the program to help his Uncle Joe in Montezuma. Miles ran a query through RealServe on Vigo, Parke and Vermillion Counties. He detailed the search to see which agents had done what production within the past 12 months. He clicked on the search button and the stats popped up. 'Hmm,' Miles thought. 'Too many – need to refine the criteria.' Miles refined the search to 3 to 4 bedroom homes (since Uncle Joe's house was a 4 bedroom home), then rearranged the order by broker and clicked. 'Ninety-four properties, that is enough,' thought Miles.

He printed off the screen.

There were 94 transactions represented by 14 brokers. Miles spent the next 30 minutes computing the statistics associated with those transactions: the average days on market, the average list-to-sales price, the average price range, then compared the stats of the top agents who worked for the top selling brokers.

He saved the agent production values, then downloaded the data onto a spreadsheet.

'Hmmm. Very interesting,' thought Miles as he looked at the agent production in west-central Indiana.

Miles picked up his phone to call his Uncle Joe as he beamed at the new information.

"Uncle Joe?" said Miles.

"Hello, is this Miles?" asked Joe.

"Yes, it's me, Uncle Joe. I wanted to get back to you about our talk the other day," started Miles.

"Oh, you're going to list the house, right?"

"Not exactly, but I have come up with a way to help you out," said Miles.

"How's that?" asked Joe.

"Uncle Joe, I just ran off some real interesting information specific to your area out there in western Indiana. I think I might be able to help you with the sale of your home, but in a different way. I am going to be your advocate and help you hire another broker to sell your home," Miles explained.

Over the next few minutes Miles told his uncle how he would contact three of the top producers in the area in and around Montezuma. Uncle Joe's home was the prize and most listing agents would like to have another listing. Miles would disclose to each of the three agents that it would be a competitive process, that there would be other agents involved in the competition for the contract.

Intrigued by the idea, Uncle Joe accepted. "And you'll sit there with me for each presentation?" asked Uncle Joe

"I'll be there for each one, Uncle Joe," replied Miles.

"But how are you going to get paid?" asked Uncle Joe.

"I do get paid, Uncle Joe. The agent who earns the right to list your home will pay me a fee, a percentage of the commission that he earns. My service really doesn't cost you anything since that fee is part of the commission. In a way, I am earning my fee by doing this work for you. Does that explain it to you well enough?"

"I think so," replied Uncle Joe, although his voice was a little unsure.

"You know you can ask me anything if you don't understand something, Uncle Joe," said Miles.

The Fishy Side of Real Estate

The Drive West

June 30, 2007

Miles was headed out to Montezuma early on a Saturday morning. The CD player was blasting the lead guitar solo of Pajama People, a Zappa classic. His car whisked through an empty downtown, the windows down, the intricate notes of Frank's lead guitar darting between complex drum patterns and the accompanying xylophone riffs: the notes ricocheting off the buildings that lined downtown Washington Street.

He admired the Capitol and headed past the Indiana State Museum, the NCAA headquarters and White River Gardens and then over the unremarkable White River. He took a long look at the zoo, trying to see some of the animals, but there were none in view. There were plenty of cars in the zoo parking lot, but no sign of life. He drove through the inner city, past railroad tracks west on Washington which is really the National Road (the first highway to go across the United States from the Atlantic to the Pacific Ocean) past the old grounds of Central State Hospital. Miles looked at the ancient cast iron fence that bordered the unkempt grounds. The State of Indiana had built the facility in the 1840s and for many years it was where authorities sent 'the crazy people' – those who might have had debilitating mental diseases or other maladies – to live out their lives. High weeds and scrap trees cluttered the once magnificent fence line as Miles imagined the poor souls who ended up there. Now it was a place for ghosts. Maybe the cluttered fence line helped keep them in, Miles thought as he drove by.

US 40 turns southwest just past Central State and then intersects with Rockville Road or US 36. It was about 90 minutes to Montezuma straight out Rockville Road from this point, out of the city, through the small county towns, over Raccoon Lake – once you got far enough west, US 36 became the Ernie Pyle Memorial Highway.

Miles adjusted the rearview mirror to keep the morning sun out of his eyes. The road was devoid of traffic. Miles recalled his discussion with Uncle Joe, who was happy to have Miles involved with the sale of his home.

Miles had called and spoken with each of the three agents who had been selected. He set the individual meetings two hours apart, beginning at ten in the morning. Miles made it clear to the agents that they would be doing their normal listing presentation within a 90 minute window. He also made it clear that there would be other agents vying for the listing. In other words, may the best listing presentation win!

It had been over a month since Miles had first spoken with his uncle about the idea, and Miles was intrigued to see how the listing presentations would go. Each individual agent was happy to have Miles sit in: after all, he was a fellow colleague, and, as he had explained, his attendance was only in consultation (plus the referral fee he was earning). Uncle Joe would get the benefit of Miles' expertise. Miles explained to Uncle Joe that his level of understanding would improve, helping him make better decisions regarding the sale of his home.

And although it wasn't a lot of money, Miles didn't care, he was achieving the greater goal of helping his uncle and that gave him more satisfaction than the eventual referral check. He imagined what the meetings with the other listing agents would be like. It made the time pass more quickly.

Miles crossed Raccoon Lake. He stuck his arm out the window to feel the air and drove across the bridge where the lake was on both sides of the car. The water relaxed him. In his new role as facilitator, he knew that he would be working like a real deckhand, chumming the bait, cleaning the deck, getting people beer; there would be no fishing for a deckhand just helping others navigate the waters.

The light was red at the intersection of US 41 and US 36. Miles was behind a pickup truck. He grabbed his cell phone and pressed a button to call Uncle Joe. "Hello," said Uncle Joe.

"Uncle Joe, it's me Miles. I'll be there in about 15 minutes."

"Been waitin' all week for you to get here," said Uncle Joe.

Miles drove toward Montezuma. He always thought the name was weird for a tiny town. Miles knew a little about the great Aztec warrior, but he had no idea why anyone would name a town of 200 people after a hero from Mexico. 'Wonder who the dude was who chose that name?' Miles thought to himself. 'Some guy must have gotten off a barge with a bottle of tequila and set up camp. Maybe it was some sort of revenge.'

The country road was familiar now, bringing back memories of his youth in full force. Miles smelled sweet honeysuckle only to be interrupted moments later by the stench of road kill. Miles tried not to look at the mangled animal in the middle of the road. He noticed three large turkey buzzards circling overhead.

Uncle Joe's was just up ahead; Miles swung in the driveway, thinking about the time he was 11 years old and Uncle Joe had let him drive the old jeep – it was always the same memory. He remembered that first encounter and now he had that same sense of exhilaration as he ambled up the driveway and onto a parking pad. He pulled up to Uncle Joe's 2000 El Dorado.

Miles honked the horn letting Uncle Joe know he was there. He always honked the horn when he arrived at Uncle Joe's.

Uncle Joe was outside, knee bent in the garden, which was growing but had no yield – too early in the summer. Uncle Joe pushed himself up. He had been pulling weeds.

Miles got out of his car. He hugged Joe at the sidewalk. Peonies lined the walkway. The flowers were all gone but were still leafy.

"Thanks for coming out, Miles," said Uncle Joe.

They went inside the 1920s bungalow style home. It was two minutes after nine.

They went into the living room. The table had been cleared.

"Want some coffee, Miles?" asked Joe.

"Sure," said Miles. "Are you ready for this, Uncle Joe?"

"Ready as I'll ever be," he stated.

The hours flew by that Saturday morning and just like clockwork, the day progressed as planned. Each agent arrived on time. Each did a good presentation. Each seemed genuinely interested in getting the listing. The market was good, even in this part of the country. It was 3 pm and Miles opened the refrigerator and pulled out a cold can of grape pop.

"Want anything, Uncle Joe?" said Miles as he turned to look at Joe, keeping the refrigerator door open.

"Nah," Joe replied as he leafed through some of the presentation materials the agents had left.

Miles walked back to the table and pulled out a chair. "Was that interesting or what?" asked Miles, applying that statement to the collective sessions they had both witnessed.

"Interesting as shit," said Uncle Joe.

Miles was happy. Uncle Joe only used the word 'shit' when something was interesting.

"Was there any agent that stood out over another?" Miles asked. He had his own ideas about which agent did well but he was interested in Uncle Joe's untainted opinion.

"The best one, hands down, was the second agent, Sarah Chapman from Camp Realty. She really seemed to know what she was talking about and I liked the way the company markets the property. I wasn't aware a real estate company did all that to advertise the home. I liked her so much that I wrote her name down as she was speaking. Did you think she was good, Miles?"

"Each of the agents was good in their own way," Miles stated accurately, since he was always careful about how he said things, especially when talking about other agents. "But what's important is how you feel, Uncle Joe. There is a lot to consider from the information we got today. Giving you some time to digest it will be a good thing." Miles said that because he had to head back for a dinner engagement in Indianapolis.

Miles began organizing some of the papers. "I need to get back home, but I will be calling you soon. We'll talk about the agents again and then when you have decided, I will contact the agents about who is getting the listing. Then you can handle it from there. How does that sound?"

"Fine with me," replied Joe. "I know who I'm gonna pick anyway."

"Give it a day or two, then we'll talk," said Miles as he stood up to clear off the table. "That was really interesting for me, too."

Miles wrapped things up, talked about a few family issues, then hugged his Uncle Joe goodbye. After the hug, Uncle Joe said, "Miles, you remember that catfish we saw on the Wabash when you were a little tyke?"

"Like it was yesterday, Uncle Joe," Miles said.

The two walked outside, the weather still beautiful and warm. A tiny, iridescent blue bird whizzed by.

"Indigo blue bunting," recited Joe pointing toward the path the bird had taken, "They fly all the way up from Central America. Beautiful, aren't they?"

"A lot prettier than a catfish!" Miles joked.

They both laughed. Miles got in his car, fired the engine and headed out the driveway. Uncle Joe waved goodbye.

Miles ambled out onto the country road and headed back. Fifteen minutes later he was headed over the Raccoon Bridge where the lake was on both sides of the car. Then it happened. Like a beam from outer space that zapped the wheels of imagination, something shot off like a firework in Miles' head. It was an idea.

"That's it!" he yelled out loud. "That's it!"

What dawned on Miles was this: He had created a business model, almost by accident, that was an improvement over the current practice. The consulting service he had done for Uncle Joe dovetailed perfectly with the service of representing buyers. If he no longer listed houses and instead, worked as a consultant for sellers, then he would eliminate the conflict of interest that arises when an agent represents both the buyer and seller. This eliminated *any* chance of limited agency. 'Wow, this is good, this is a major improvement,' Miles thought to himself.

Then his enthusiasm waned as he thought about the Berlin couple. The closing was in ten days. Even though there had been no issues, and the transaction had breezed through, he still felt a slight, ethical pang of remorse. Had he done anything wrong?

Miles turned up the radio for some needed interference.

Two days later, Miles called and talked to Uncle Joe and he was ready to sign with Ms. Chapman. Miles called the other agents to thank them for their effort and time, and told them that Camp Realtors had been awarded the listing contract. He spoke with Sarah Chapman of Camp Realty who was delighted to get the listing contract. Miles faxed Camp Realty a referral contract, which entitled him to the referral fee.

Sarah sold Uncle Joe's house for list price the following week. Everybody was happy. Especially Uncle Joe.

The Closing

July 9, 2007

Everybody was on time for the Miller-Berlin closing. It was being held at Hinterland Title Company up on 82nd street. This was the main headquarters for the company closing the transaction for 901 Buckle Street. The office overlooked a manmade lake to the south. It was 11 am sharp on a Monday morning.

Marty Miller showed up in a suit. Melanie and Andrew Berlin were fashionable. Miles wore a flowered Hawaiian shirt. It was an odd fashion choice, but Miles, who normally dressed professionally, always wore a flowered shirt for closings. He never would explain the reason he did. He just always showed up for closings informally.

They were all standing in the lobby when a woman approached the group. She recognized Miles and knew it was the Miller-Berlin closing. She nodded to Miles. Debbie had participated in many closings with Miles over the years.

"Good morning," she began. "My name is Debbie Truman and I'll be closing your transaction this morning. You must be Andrew and Melanie," she shook hands with them then turned to Marty Miller. "You must be Mr. Miller. Good morning!" She shook Marty's hand then motioned them to follow her back to a closing room.

They all entered the closing room. Debbie set a thick file on the table and motioned to Melanie and Andrew to sit on her right, and the seller, Marty Miller, to sit on her left. Debbie took the seat which was closest to the door.

Miles came in last and shut the door behind him. Miles sat toward the other end of the table. He had the best view of the water.

"Looks like we got everybody here!" Debbie said with enthusiasm, twenty five percent of which was fake. She pulled the thick file in front of her. "Let's get started."

Debbie began by asking the buyers and seller for their driver's licenses. Miles was looking out the window over the calm lake. He heard them and even said something, but the water began to entrance him.

He was slipping back to 1980. His mind replayed a quiet morning on the Gulf of Mexico when Miles was invited to fish on a 55' Hatteras fishing boat. He didn't have to work on this particular expedition; it was a pleasure trip for him. It wasn't often that he got to pleasure fish, but this was one of those lucky times when he got to relax, as someone else would be handling the duties of the deckhand today.

They had left Port Aransas early that morning – two hours before the sun came up. The captain had charted a course toward the Flower Garden Banks, a coral reef zone off the coast of Texas and Louisiana about 110 miles from Port Aransas.

The sun had just come up, casting its nascent glow over brightening sky and water: both had transformed from black to blue, although entirely different shades. Miles was climbing the ladder up to the bridge when he saw it – it was a current change. In the middle of the Gulf you run into it sometimes, and now, as the sun bled over the horizon, everyone on the boat could see the distinct line between the dark bluish water on one side, and a flat, dull green on the other. It is a strange phenomenon that most people never see. The stark difference in colors means there are different water temperatures on either side of the current change and those differences attract sea creatures. If you work at sea, a current change is well known as a good place to catch fish. Miles called to the captain, a weathered veteran named Charlie. "Hey Captain, look at that current change! Think we should drop the lines?"

"Absolutely, Miles!" replied Captain Charlie.

Miles assisted the deckhand with getting the bait ready. He quickly assembled four monster reels outfitted with 200 lb test fishing line: they would be fishing for trophy fish today. He had prepared fishing lines a hundred times and now he was going to get an opportunity to fish; maybe it would finally be his moment in the captain's chair.

The captain angled the Hatteras along the current change, trolling about six knots. The boat rolled along the line, the diesel engines gurgling. The boat idled along for several minutes running on one side of the line or the other. There was a feeling of anticipation in the air. The sun became brighter as the waves rolled.

And then it hit as quick as a car collision. One of the lines was screaming and Miles grabbed the flexing pole. They quickly helped him into the chair and strapped him in. He held on for dear life. The reel whined and the line flew out. Miles let the fish take the line out – he could not fight something that big. The thick rod bent double. He had hooked a monster and it would be the ultimate tug of war game, but with a fish on the other end much bigger than him, this would require patience.

Miles' tan arms were rigid. He had been letting slack out for nearly ten minutes. He arched his back and used all the force of his legs to combat the beast below. 'What have I hooked?' Miles wondered.

Then it broke the water like a missile shot out of a silo. It exploded into the air almost 10 feet. It was a marlin.

Captain Charlie screamed, "A black marlin, Miles! A huge one, maybe 500, 600 pounds!"

The fish was making another run. Miles let the line drag. The rod bent. Miles held on.

"Goddamn, big fish!" grunted Miles.

Everyone's attention was on the fight. Miles had hooked a black marlin, which was quite rare in the Gulf of Mexico. Miles was getting tired. He was sweating it out by himself. Everyone was looking at him.

"Land that motherfucker!" screamed Bobby, the deckhand, as he steadied himself by the ladder, his other hand on a gaff.

The black marlin broke the surface again, this time much closer to the boat. The glistening fish landed on its side sending a wave of water onto the boat.

"Did you fucking see that!" screamed Bobby.

The black marlin made another run for its life.

Miles held on to the pole with both hands. He could not even think about reeling.

"Fucking aye!" screamed Miles, his arms throbbing, his back aching. He leaned back with all his might.

Sometimes a fight between a man and a huge fish is not even. Sometimes the line breaks or sometimes the lure dislodges, and every once in a while, the man wins and battles the hooked fish into exhaustion. This was the case with Miles. His perseverance, after nearly an hour of fighting, finally paid off. The black marlin could no longer fight. He had given up.

Bobby leaned over to gaff and secure the gargantuan fish and drag it to the side of the boat. Tag and release wasn't a consideration back then. You brought the fish back to port, then hoisted it up on a hook to weigh it and have pictures taken with it. It was a trophy fish destined for a wall in some fancy country club. They would throw that fish in the deep freeze and have it mounted someday – it was the ultimate trophy.

Miles peered over at the prize, a black marlin. He looked at its black eye. He had won.

"There. That's the last signature I need," said Debbie, the closing agent. "Let me make some copies and I'll be back in a few moments."

The transaction of 901 Buckle Street went very smoothly. Smooth deals were not all that common – something usually popped up in most transactions that caused tension; a poor inspection that might cost the seller more in repair dollars, an appraisal that came in below what the buyer had offered, or something that a buyer or seller perceives that could unbalance the deal from a monetary or ethical perspective. This was the ebb and flow of emotional and monetary involvement for buyers and sellers: the rush of making the money or the despair of losing it: the sense of being jilted by not having all of the facts disclosed.

But it didn't happen here. Everybody was all smiles; the transaction sailed along without a hitch. Everybody was happy.

Everybody was smiling. "That was a piece of cake!" cried Marty.

Deals like that make real estate agents happy, and Miles kept calm, but inside, he felt the joy of a big payday, a monster trophy. Andrew Berlin noticed Miles' detached look and asked. "Miles, everything ok?"

Miles suddenly realized where he was and responded instantaneously with a gush of optimism, "Just great. And it looks like you all did your duty to the letter of the contract which makes my job easier. It has been a pleasure and an honor to serve both of you."

Miles was serious about this and the clients felt his sincere empathy.

"Miles, you have been terrific," said Melanie.

"I can't believe it went so quickly," responded Marty. They all chatted about the house for a few more minutes, then the closing agent entered with a file.

Standing in the doorway, smiling, she said, "OK, we have copies for everybody!" She passed out the neat folders which had the Hinterland company logo emblazoned across the front. She handed the last file to Miles. "Good job, Miles," she said quietly. Miles took the folder and opened it up. Inside was an envelope. Miles opened the flap to peer inside. A check made out to Trinity Real Estate for $22,750.

Miles was ambivalent about the amount. His latent guilt took a backseat to the closing celebration. He closed the file quickly and stood up.

"Thanks again, everybody," Debbie cheerfully announced.

Everyone stood up. The closing agent left the room first, then Miles, Melanie, Andrew and Marty.

The clients group-hugged Miles, thanking him for all he did. It took him a little by surprise, but Miles was good on his feet.

Critical Coffee

July 30, 2007

It was a banner year for real estate and the top producing agents had much to cheer about.

Miles was driving to a Starbucks before going into work on a Monday morning. He was meeting Gary Paulson, a fellow agent who worked for Trinity, but from the northeast office.

They sat in a corner sipping regular coffee.

"The concept has potential, Gary," began Miles.

Gary and Miles had gone through the same Trinity training class when they started their real estate careers. Even though they worked at different offices, they remained friends. They were like-minded, but Gary was more conservative.

"It happened by accident, sort of," Miles began. "I had planned to refer a listing out in western Indiana for my Uncle Joe who lives in Montezuma – you know how family is – and instead of just making a few calls, I really went the extra mile for him and actually sat in each listing presentation – all three of them."

"You did what?" Gary interrupted. "You drove out to Montezuma to listen to three agents? That's overkill isn't, Miles?"

"No, it wasn't. I mean it was really interesting. My uncle is pretty sharp, but having me there to fill in the gaps or to ask for clarification on some points during the interviews was really helpful, at least that's what my Uncle Joe said," Miles stated.

"But you're just getting a referral fee, right? Is it worth all the work?" asked Gary.

"Here's the thing, Gary. From an ethical consideration," said Miles, "something dawned on me as I was driving back from Montezuma and it was this: if you couple the services of being a seller consultant with that of a buyer's agent, the union of those services eliminates the conflict of interest that can arise from limited agency. Gary, you know what I mean?"

"You know it doesn't happen that often, Miles," stated Gary. "And you would give up listing homes to accommodate that idea?"

"Well, with the consulting idea, it's impossible to misrepresent either the buyer or seller from an agency standpoint. And since the consultant does his work before the home comes on the market, the consulting concept avoids the pitfalls of limited agency. I mean, it says so right in the State disclosure that with dual agency the agent cannot give either the buyer or seller a competitive advantage during the course of the transaction – and that is verbatim, Gary," Miles said with emphasis.

"Think about the dilemma that every agent faces when he engages both the buyer and seller in the same transaction: some of our agency attributes can become compromised! If the State disclosure says that you cannot give *either* client a contractual advantage, then somebody might get shortchanged. That situation already erodes the attribute of disclosure, because you cannot disclose anything to either client that would provide an advantage. You can no longer obey the client, because you may violate the code by providing accurate information that must now be withheld! Where's the loyalty to the client?" Miles said loudly. "We are doing less than we can, but we're getting paid twice as much. Doesn't that make perfect, ethical sense, Gary?!" he said sarcastically as his face turned red.

"Ok, ok, I get it. But you really cut your profitability when you only represent buyers," commented Gary.

"Forget the money for a moment, Gary! What about our duty to the client? How can you take that money knowing you might have compromised the deal for either one of your clients?" Miles asked strongly.

"Nobody in real estate would go for it," said Gary. "Taking away the right to represent both parties would cut deeply into some brokers' pockets."

"Yeah, it's pretty apparent that ethics take a back seat to profit, but I guess that's the way America operates, Gary," Miles said, whining somewhat. He finished his coffee. "I had a closing a couple weeks ago where I represented both the buyer and the seller. Everything went smoothly, there weren't any problems with the transaction, but in the end I don't think I did my best job."

"What exactly do you mean, Miles?"

"It's an ethical issue. I did everything according to the rules, but in the end my hands were tied. I felt they overpaid for the home I listed, but there was nothing I could do about it, and that bugs me," Miles said pointedly.

"Geez, Miles, is it bugging you that much?" asked Gary.

"I guess it is, now that I think about it," said Miles.

"Then why don't you do something about it?"

"Like what?"

"Maybe you could start your own real estate firm and use that concept you were telling me about," Gary replied.

"Now that's not a bad idea!"

They finished their coffee and stood up to leave.

"Guess we better get to work," Gary stated.

"Yeah, there's lots to do," said Miles.

They walked out of the Starbucks and headed to their cars. Miles got into his car, started it up and thought about the idea of starting his own real estate firm. Miles thought the concept of eliminating any potential conflict of interest was a worthy pursuit.

The Office Party

September 21, 2007

Trinity was having a function on the north side of town. Everybody was having a good year. The agents were closing deals, profits were at near record highs, and the management even got bonuses earlier than usual.

The Trinity principals decided to throw a party at one of the swanky restaurants near the main office. Management had reserved one of the large banquet rooms at the restaurant. The room was packed with agents and managers. The room was buzzing with conversation. It was late afternoon Friday.

Miles was nursing a martini, listening to Kat Thrasher discuss her listings with two other agents.

"I have about had it with my sellers over in Eagle Cove," she complained. "Their house is not selling because they have it listed too high. I've had plenty of showings, but they want to blame me because there has not been one offer!"

"Comes with the territory," said Dean Bower, a north side Trinity agent who teamed up with his wife, Sherry.

Sherry chimed in, "You know, sellers always blame the listing agent if they don't get a sale right away."

"It didn't help that two homes sold on their street in the past few weeks," Kat said, "but those homes were priced closer to market value, which sure makes it easier to get an offer. Half the feedback from the buyers' agent comments includes that the home is overpriced, but that doesn't seem to have any impact. My sellers won't drop the price!"

Miles interjected, "Every seller wants to maximize the net proceeds. That's all they care about."

"You're right about that Miles!" Dean said.

"These days, sellers seem to get about any price they want. Appraisers seem to rubber stamp about every deal. It makes the sellers believe that they can get any price for their home, unless of course, it is *grossly* overpriced," Kat replied, exaggerating the word 'grossly' with some facial animation.

The discussion was a microcosm for the entire real estate industry. Over the past few years, the government had relaxed the rules for borrowing money. It really began with the Clinton administration, when they felt that every American should become a home owner. Almost anyone could qualify for a mortgage. It seemed you needed a pulse and a credit card to get approved: buyers, even those with poor credit, were qualifying for loans that required little money down. Even the higher interest rates that accompanied these higher risk loans weren't weighed as a factor; in fact people didn't care what they were paying. Maybe people thought that loan paid itself back.

Maybe people thought it was real estate fantasy. Like watching the shootout at the OK Corral, the observers thought it was entertainment until they realized it wasn't a movie – it was the next great real estate investment. They woke up and there they were in the dusty streets of the old west, bullets whizzing by in all directions. People didn't know they were about to be involved in the shootout. Most of them didn't even know how to use a gun.

Kat turned to Miles and asked, "How are your listings doing downtown?"

"Not bad," Miles said. "The historic districts have increased in value pretty well, but there aren't many families that move in."

"That's because no one wants their kids to go to the inner city public schools," Kat shot back. They all knew she was right.

"There are other options besides public schools," Miles replied. "There are some pretty good charter schools and some excellent private schools that are just as good as the suburbs. Besides, the lesson in diversity is free!"

Miles was being sarcastic because he knew most agents would never even consider showing any upwardly mobile families inner city homes: it was 'steering' – the guiding of home buyers to or away from particular neighborhoods – at its finest. But among the real estate professionals, the downtown area was pretty much off limits for most families. Of course, there were those clients that desired the alternative lifestyle, but those people usually didn't have any kids, and if they did, the numbers didn't amount to much. Miles had a strong opinion about this since he and his wife had raised their two girls in one of the historic districts, and they had managed to figure out the educational issue in the inner city of Indianapolis.

Dean chimed in, "Miles, I don't know why you live downtown when you could be living in Carmel and having your kids attend one of the best public schools in the state." Dean and Sherry had raised their children in Carmel. Miles didn't mention that one of the Bower kids had been convicted of dealing cocaine, but this was not the moment to mention that.

"Well, we're pretty happy downtown and I think we're going to stay there," Miles said.

Amid the noise, the tinkling sound of a fork against a glass sounded. It quieted the crowd.

"Welcome everybody!" began the owner of Trinity, Jerry Leach. "We thought we'd gather everybody this afternoon for a little celebration in recognition of the fine work you all have done so far this year."

Jerry Leach went on to recognize those agents whose production had exceeded the company's expectations. Numerous awards, gift certificates and plaques were handed out. Even Miles was recognized for his trail blazing efforts in the inner city.

Twenty minutes later Jerry wrapped up the presentation. "I want to personally thank you all for coming this afternoon and we hope that you continue to achieve success in this great market! Thanks to all for a job well done, and please continue the celebration!"

The room was back to buzzing with real estate conversation.

Miles had refreshed his martini and was back to talking with the same group. Kat and Dean were discussing limited agency, referring to a deal Kat had closed recently in one of the nicer subdivisions in Carmel.

Kat had represented both the buyer and seller in the transaction and Dean was discussing the pitfalls of dual agency.

Dean asked, "Kat, did you ever feel at any point during the deal, like you had compromised either client?" Miles was listening closely, remembering his own dilemma with the Berlin couple.

"Well, I did everything I was supposed to do, according to our office policies and the State disclosure on limited agency," Kat said.

Miles jumped in, "Kat, did you feel, at any point, that you had done any disservice to either your buyers or sellers?"

Kat didn't respond immediately, but rather, cast a hard glance at Miles. Her eyes narrowed somewhat. "*I* said that *I* did what *I* was supposed to do, Miles." Her tone was rougher – she had audibly said the word "I" louder than the other words – and she realized it, making her shift gears into a sappier sweetness. "You know, Miles, I always try to do my best, for me and Trinity."

Miles knew he was pressing a button, but his own dilemma made him push on.

"I do too, Kat," Miles began, "but don't you think we run into situations where we are absolutely compromising our ability to represent either client in a limited agency situation?"

Kat glared at Miles. "What is the big deal, Miles? You know we do *exactly* what Trinity wants us to do in disclosing company policy, so what is the fucking deal?" Kat's claws were out. She didn't like being cornered, especially by a fellow company agent.

But Miles didn't back down because he was at odds with himself, with his own experience, and now he wanted Kat to come clean, to see if she would weigh the issue and discuss the ethics of the matter. Would the money trump ethics? He wanted to know badly because he could not reconcile the issue on his own. He felt like he was on an island, alone in the middle of the ocean.

"Kat, I closed a deal not that long ago where I know for an absolute fact that the buyers were fucked." Miles didn't use the word fuck very often, and everyone there knew that. "I was at an Open House where the buyers were hooked and I was helpless to do anything about it, and I felt terrible." Miles was not holding back. "There was nothing I could do to help the buyers in a situation where my negotiating skills were hogtied!" Miles had actually yelled the word, which was unusual for him but two martinis had forced it out.

Miles went on, "I really felt like I had done an injustice to the buyers."

"And why was that?" snapped Kat.

"Because I knew that the home was worth less than what they were offering and there was nothing I could do about it. The state disclosure states that I must only disclose to the buyer what price the seller will accept – and I cannot say it is one dollar less! We closed the deal and the buyers never knew anything about the fact that they had paid more for the house than what it was worth," Miles said.

Nobody said anything. All three realtors looked at Miles numbly. They knew he was right, but he was treading on an area that didn't need to be treaded on. The silence was obvious in that small group even though there was plenty of chatter in the room. The conversation ended on that odd note.

The Great Rift

September 21, 2007

Miles left the company party and headed to his car. He was one of the first to leave. It was the silence of the previous conversation with his fellow colleagues that had pushed him out, as though he had fallen overboard from a boat and into the sea.

Miles was driving home. No music, no radio, no nothing except what was on his mind: the fact that he had made an ethical point which made sense and was defendable. And there was nobody backing him up.

It was then, only a few minutes after leaving the company party with two martinis in his system, that Miles thought he could do better using his own improved business model for transacting residential property. He was 99% sure.

Miles was thinking deeply. His mind was swimming in the dichotomy of ethics. He knew that the majority of his realtor brethren were only interested in one thing: the money. The money was more important than anything else. He dwelled on it because it was a choice of right versus wrong. He wrestled with it like a 50 pound kingfish on a ten pound test line.

Then, like awakening from a long nap at sea, Miles made up his mind: he would venture out on his own. But he would move carefully. He would do his homework first, before making any moves that might cost him. He had made the decision: he would merge the concept of the consulting method – that meant he would no longer list homes – with the full agency relationship of representing buyers. This idea would eliminate any conflict of interest that might arise from the compromising nature of limited agency.

Then Miles drifted back to an experience he had 15 years ago in the Caribbean. He had gone to the Grand Caymans, a group of three small islands stuck between the Yucatan Peninsula in the west and Cuba from the east. This area is where the Caribbean meets the Gulf.

The Gulf of Mexico, to the north, is like a shallow bowl: the depth is very gradual. You can take a boat three miles off Port Aransas and the water is only 30 feet deep. But on Grand Cayman Island, the north shore reef in the Caribbean drops off like the Grand Canyon less than 50 yards from the beach. The color line where the two areas meet is vividly noticeable in the water: from the shoreline there's light, aquamarine water that is crystal clear until the color suddenly changes to a deep and dark, bluish-purple color; the place where the depth of the ocean falls off the map.

Miles thought about the first time he snorkeled in Grand Cayman. He dove into the sparkling sea water and swam the short distance to the reef, toward the dark, purple line. He swam out over the dark water and then he looked down. Even though he was in crystalline water, the depth was unfathomable. The sun's rays diminished after 100 feet or more into the sea, and below that, the darkness fell for thousands of feet. Miles floated above it, a tiny speck over the great, deep, water-filled canyon. Miles could see that the reef wall was encrusted with spectacular coral, sea fans, colorful striped fish, and other creatures. And beyond the wall, as far down as you could see into the darkness, the edge disappearing into the void beyond, the black abyss. Then he shuddered. Suddenly he was afraid, very afraid. He was confused by his fear. A practical guy, Miles knew he would not fall over the edge, nor would it be some terrifying creature from below that would come up to snatch him. What was scaring him? Then quickly, Miles began swimming back to the safety of shallow water. In fifteen seconds he was standing in four feet of salt water, his toes wedged into the firm white sand, his heart pounding. What was he afraid of? He wasn't sure.

Miles gripped the steering wheel, remembering that first visit to Grand Cayman. He was sure his idea would fly. His mind raced with excitement. He could be ready by January first.

○
○
○

The Day of Affirmation

October 26, 2007

Miles was at his home office opening a letter from one of the local law offices in town. Over the past several weeks, Miles had performed his due diligence for the new concept by contacting two local law firms to consider a legal opinion on his new idea. Even though he knew his concept improved the clarity of agency and eliminated the conflict of interest associated with limited agency, Miles still felt having a legal opinion would give the idea a solid foundation from which to grow. He still had not told anyone about his imminent decision to leave Trinity.

Miles slit the envelope using an old brass opener he had bought from a yard sale. It was from the defunct Indianapolis Office Furniture company which had a display room on the main floor of the Chamber of Commerce Building. Old printing on the opener had the telephone number as: 'RILEY 2221.' Back in the day, telephone prefixes were named after parts of the city, and if you dialed the local operator, a caller would include the name in the number.

Miles opened the letter from the firm of Curlee, Cohen & Casey, a medium sized firm downtown. It didn't take long for Miles to read it. It said:

"Dear Mr. Vincent,

Thank you for your inquiry about obtaining a legal opinion on your business concept, however, at this time, we find a conflict of interest that arises internally and we must decline our services. Please consider our services for any other legal issues that may arise.

Respectfully,
Curlee, Cohen & Casey."

This was the second letter that he had received with the same message. 'What is the deal?' Miles asked himself. But he already knew the answer. The problem was, introducing a real estate concept could alter public perception about the manner in which real estate transactions should be performed. For any firm that had a large real estate company as a client, Miles' idea could be considered a threat, and at the very least, an annoyance, so it is understandable that there would be some fallout among his colleagues.

But the consulting concept was a better idea because the consultant had no agenda to get a listing contract signed; the role of the consultant was to be an advocate for the seller, to help the seller understand the process completely, and to help them negotiate the best contract possible. On the back side of the sale, the consultant was prepared to wear another hat and become the buyer's agent for the new purchase. The bonus to the buyer is that the agent can guarantee – even promise – 100% buyer's representation during the purchase of the new residence. That dynamic is an improvement over the current practice where it is allowed for the same agent to represent a buyer and seller in the same transaction. The real estate industry doesn't really want consumers understanding the rules of agency anyway. A good consumer understanding of agency attributes would complicate the existing culture. And worse, that prize at the end of the line, that doubling of potential income, would vanish. Deep inside his mind, Miles knew that was the crux of the matter. His thinking leapfrogged. He wanted to make things clear and less complicated.

He picked up his phone and went into his directory and scrolled down until he found Jim Richardson, a past client and independent attorney who worked in Broad Ripple. Jim was an old hippie, but a good attorney, and Miles knew he wouldn't be getting a rejection letter from Jim.

He pressed the call button.

"Law Office," a gravelly voice said on the second ring.

"Jim, hey, it's Miles Vincent calling," Miles spoke.

"Miles, my man!" shouted Jim. "How are you doing?"

"Fine thanks, Jim. Hope you're doing well, too," Miles said. "I was wondering if you might do some work for me, maybe write a document that validates a real estate business concept that I want to use."

"Now say what?" Jim answered, a little puzzled.

Miles took the next ten minutes to explain to Jim the consulting concept and the reason behind wanting a legal opinion on the start-up.

"Well it seems clear cut to me," Jim stated. "You actually have less liability than all the other real estate brokers. Because your idea eliminates limited agency, there is much less chance, in fact, no chance that you find yourself complicating matters while representing the buyer and seller in the same transaction. Pretty good, Miles. Pretty clean, too."

"Think I can drop my Errors and Omissions insurance?" asked Miles, half joking, half not.

"I don't know that I would do that, Miles," Jim replied. "There are other areas beyond the scope of agency where the insurance may offer some protection."

"I was just asking," Miles stated. "Jim, you know I'm planning to go out on my own soon," Miles began, "and I think this new concept is important and it feels like the right thing to do, but I just wanted to get a lawyer's opinion."

Jim laughed as he thought about what Miles was proposing to do. He laughed because he admired what Miles was doing. Jim's humor emanated from a thought, a comparison to a famous speech given by Robert F. Kennedy at Cape Town University in 1966.

"Miles, you remember that speech Bobby Kennedy made in Cape Town, South Africa in 1966?" Jim asked. "It was during the civil rights era and I remember reading it in law school at IU. The Day of Affirmation speech – you know it?"

"No, should I?" asked Miles, a little embarrassed that he couldn't reference Jim's point.

"Yeah, Miles, you should know about that speech. The reason is that Kennedy's speech is analogous to your situation," Jim said.

"What do you mean?" asked Miles.

"In that speech, RFK quotes an Italian philosopher who said, *'There is nothing more difficult to take in hand, more perilous to conduct, or more uncertain in its success than to take the lead in the introduction of a new order of things.'* He made that quote, then he went on to describe the challenges that await people who do ruffle feathers, that go against the grain – people like you!" Jim said loudly and laughing a bit.

"What kind of challenges was Kennedy talking about?" asked Miles.

"Most of this stuff was toward the end of his speech – and he was really addressing apartheid in South Africa – but Kennedy went on to outline the dangers and pitfalls that come to people like you, people who try to change things that are deeply ingrained. One pitfall was 'futility', the notion that you cannot change something that you believe is wrong, so that sense of futility will keep you from pursuing what you believe. Another pitfall was 'expediency', and by that Kennedy meant, and I quote, *"of those who say that hopes and beliefs must bend before immediate necessities."* Jim was happy to find an apt analogy for what he thought was one of the best speeches ever made by an American. "What he meant by that… was… just a second, Miles." Jim swiveled on his chair and reached behind him to pull out an old, worn book. Jim flipped to a tabbed page and said, "I'm going to read this to you, Miles," as he put on reading glasses. "This is what Bobby Kennedy said in the speech about making his point on expediency, remember, this is 1966 – *"But if there is one thing that President Kennedy stood for that touched the most profound feeling of young people across the world, it was the belief that idealism, high aspiration and deep convictions are not incompatible with the most practical and efficient programs – that there is no basic inconsistency between ideals and realistic possibilities – no separation between the deepest desires of heart and mind and the rational application of human effort to human problems."*

"Hmmm…" was the sound Miles made over the phone.

Jim replied, "Wait, Miles, he goes on: *"It is not realistic or hardheaded to solve problems and take action unguided by ultimate moral aims and values, although we all know some who claim that it is so. In my judgment, it is thoughtless folly. For it ignores the realities of human faith and of passion and belief; forces ultimately more powerful than all of the calculations of our economists or of our generals. Of course, to adhere to standards, to idealism, to vision in the face of immediate dangers takes great courage and takes self-confidence. But we also know that those who dare to fail greatly, can never achieve greatly."* You listening to that, Miles?" asked Jim, thinking that might be proving a point too much. "Kennedy is addressing that same idealism you're professing. Is this getting through to you, Miles?"

"Yeah, Jim, I hear you loud and clear," Miles spoke.

"One of the other dangers is being timid." Jim went back to the book, "Here, Bobby goes on to say: *Few men are willing to brave the disapproval of their fellows, the censure of their colleagues, the wrath of their society. Moral courage is a rarer commodity than bravery in battle or great intelligence. Yet it is the one essential, vital quality for those who seek to change the world which yields most painfully to change."*

"Wow, that's right on!" Miles yelled.

"The fourth danger Kennedy says is 'comfort'. He says, *'the temptation to follow the easy and familiar path of personal ambition and financial success so grandly spread before those who have the privilege of an education.'*

"That hits the nail on the head, Jim," Miles replied. "I can relate to what he is saying, definitely."

"You ready to take that on, Miles?" Jim asked with some gravity.

"You ready to write me a legal opinion?" asked Miles.

The Announcement

November 1, 2007

Terry Hanover was at his desk looking over October reports. It was a few minutes before 8 am on a Monday morning. The half cup of coffee on the desk was cold. A tapping on his door interrupted his concentration. He looked up to see Miles peering his head in from the hall.

"Morning, Miles, c'mon in," Terry said. "What's up with you this morning?"

Miles walked in and sat down with hot coffee. He put the mug on Terry's desk.

"Terry," Miles began, "after a lot of thought, I have decided to leave Trinity."

Terry looked up, then took off his reading glasses. "You're doing what, Miles?" Terry was surprised, and it was a surprise given the early Monday morning fog of numbers and caffeine. Terry assumed Miles was leaving for a competitor and appeared angry. "That's just great," he said sarcastically. "And are you going to be working for anyone we know?" Terry asked while grabbing a pen.

"No, Terry, I'm not going to work for a competitor, I am going out on my own," Miles said.

The unthreatening statement let the pressure out of the room. In fact, it changed Terry's demeanor completely. "Well, what brings this change all of a sudden?" Terry inquired, pointedly.

"It's just time, I think. Been thinking about it for a while and I just think it's time to try it on my own," Miles said.

Terry was not offended that an agent would strike out on his own. All real estate agents know you have to have the big name backing you up or you didn't stand a chance. That's just the way it was.

"I admire your tenacity, Miles," even though Terry thought it was the wrong choice, because in his own mind losing a good agent meant a production loss. "Are you sure you've thought everything out?" he said with a twinge of longing.

"I have been thinking about it for a while," said Miles "and I wanted to talk to you about it first. I was planning on being ready to go by January first, if that sounds ok."

Terry knew what he had to do and it was a Trinity policy about defecting agents that made him utter the next sentence.

"Miles, you can start moving out of your office today," Terry said without emotion.

Miles sat stunned. He was frozen with shock. But it only lasted a second. "You mean now?!" he gasped.

"Company policy, Miles, and you know I don't like doing it this way," Terry commented, as Miles stood up.

"Nor do I," said Miles as he walked out of Terry's office.

PART TWO

The Fishy Side of Real Estate

More Coffee

January 10, 2008

It was a cold Thursday in Indianapolis and Miles was getting coffee at the Starbucks on the Circle. He stood in line behind ten other customers. You could see people's breath as they came through the door.

Miles had managed to find a great downtown office location on Mass Avenue back in late November. He had signed a 3-year lease on a small office and had it up and running in a matter of weeks. It had all happened so fast. He had named his small real estate start-up, Clear Choice Realtors. He felt the name offered consumers a more logical choice, a more ethical choice.

The transition from being an agent in a large franchise to being an independent broker/agent was not as difficult as he thought. During the years that Miles had worked for Trinity, he became accustomed to doing most of the work himself. Early in his career with Trinity, Miles realized that the agent did the real work. The most interaction he had with the company was when he handed a completed transaction to the secretary, who usually swiveled around in the chair to file the papers in the pending transaction file.

Miles' new office was only a few blocks away from Starbucks. He had started his office with little fanfare or advertising. He still had existing clients and a healthy stream of referral business, so he wasn't starving. But the most noticeable thing was the absence of other agents.

"Coffee Venti," Miles ordered as he stepped up next in line. "And room for cream."

"That will be two dollars, sir," the girl behind the counter replied.

Miles pulled out his money clip and peeled off three dollars. He gave the girl two and put the other one in the tip jar. He grabbed his coffee then made his way to the condiment table for cream and sugar. Then he spied one open chair next to a low table.

Across from him was an old man, who might have been a beggar. To the right of Miles was a couple in their early 30s. He was quiet for a moment listening to the noise of multiple conversations. He overheard the couple talking about a new brewery that had opened up downtown and they didn't seem to know where it was.

Miles jumped into the conversation, "The Sun King brewery is right over on College and Ohio," he replied, "just a few blocks from here."

"Oh, thanks," the woman responded, "I didn't know it was so close to here."

"Microbreweries are doing well," Miles said.

"We like them better than the massed-produced varieties," the man said.

"Me, too," Miles said. "And my name is Miles." He leaned forward across the table and shook hands.

"My name is Jim Garcia and this is my wife Nancy," Jim said.

Miles shook hands with Nancy.

"Nice to meet you both," Miles said. "Do you work downtown?

"We both do," Jim said. "We both work for Simon Properties."

"A good, local company that made it big," Miles said.

"What do you do, Miles?" asked Nancy.

"I'm a real estate agent," Miles answered.

"Oh that's interesting. Jim and I were talking about moving downtown. Do you know the downtown area?"

"Absolutely," Miles responded. "I worked for Trinity for many years, but I decided to become an independent a few months ago," he said as he reached for his wallet and took out two business cards. He handed them across the table.

"Clear Choice Realtors… hmm, never heard of it," said Jim.

"Well, the company is only a few months old, so that's not surprising," said Miles. "I haven't advertised much either."

Nancy asked, "So you work mostly downtown, Miles?"

"Well, I have lived downtown for nearly 20 years so I feel like I know the area pretty well. But I went out on my own to start a new concept in real estate."

"How are you different from the other real estate companies?" Jim asked.

"That's a good question," Miles answered. He could see he had their attention so he continued. "Last year I decided to try a new concept for sellers and now I am offering that service. I work as a consultant for sellers and I help them hire another real estate company. Does that make sense?"

Jim replied, "We have owned one other home before the one we have now, so we did use a real estate company to list the property."

"How did you find that company?" asked Miles.

"We used the same company that helped us buy it," said Nancy.

"Did you use the same agent that helped you buy the home?" Miles questioned.

"Yes, we did," they answered.

"What I do that's different is that I meet with sellers before they hire a real estate firm," Miles said. "For example, if I worked as a consultant for you, I would generate all the statistical production that real estate agents have produced in your home area. I would meet with both of you and show you which agents did what. Like how many homes they sold in your area, how long it took them to do it, and what their average list to sales price was. I bring those stats to you and we discuss the agent activity, then we compare agents on statistical productivity. One of the interesting things is that there is a big difference in job skill sets used by the agent in the representation of buyers and sellers. Just because you had a great buyer's agent representing your purchase, doesn't mean he would be an outstanding listing agent. Some agents can provide listing and selling services, but many of them are better at one or the other. Does that make sense?"

"So you don't list the home, you just help us hire someone else?" asked Nancy.

"That's right. I don't do anything else but supply the realtor stats and help sellers understand agent production. We are really trying to hone in on the best listing agents in your area. From that specific list of agents the sellers will pick three agents and one alternate. The alternate is chosen in case one of the agents doesn't want to do it," said Miles.

"Do what?" asked Nancy.

"Make their listing presentation to us. I sit in on all three listing presentations which are held at the seller's home. Most sellers like me there because I am an advocate for them and I only care about getting them the best agent at the best price," explained Miles.

"How do you get paid?" asked Jim.

"Good question, Jim. The agent who earns the listing contract must agree to pay me a referral fee if they get the listing," Miles answered.

"You said the best agent at the best price. So what did you mean by that?" asked Nancy.

"Every state in the US says that a real estate commission is a negotiable issue. Real estate firms cannot fix the commission percentage," said Miles.

"I thought it was seven percent. That's all I've ever heard," Jim said.

"That's what they want you to think it is," Miles stated. "But fixing a commission is a federal antitrust violation. The real estate broker cannot fix the commission. It is negotiable and that's the law. After we have completed all the agent interviews, I will speak with the sellers and ask them which agent they liked. Part of my service is to negotiate the commission amount. So maybe a seller liked an agent who had the higher commission. I will speak with them to see if they will come down to a more acceptable rate. A lower commission rate means sellers will put more money in their pocket! Does that make sense?"

"Oh, now I get it!" said Nancy. Her eyes had lit up and Miles noticed the visceral response. "Yeah, that's pretty cool. Does anybody else do that?" she asked.

"I think I am the only one," said Miles. He had wanted to explain the reason behind the concept, he wanted to elaborate on how the concept eliminated the vagaries of limited agency, but he knew there was not enough time.

"If you need a good buyer's agent for looking at homes downtown, I can help!" Miles said enthusiastically.

Nancy still clutched Miles' card. She looked at it. "We may give you a call. I kind of like that seller consulting. You like it too, Jim?" she asked.

"Well, it's different," Jim answered.

They all stood up, ready to move on.

"It was nice to meet you both. Please consider calling me if you need any assistance," said Miles. "And my website does a lot better job of explaining the idea!"

They all walked out into the bitter cold and waved goodbye.

Professional Standards

January 29, 2008

Miles was at his desk going through some files and reviewing home searches for his buying clients. Hometown buyers usually hibernated like bears during the winter months. Many out-of-season buyers were generated by corporate relocation jobs. Nearly all of the buyer referrals were handled by large franchise operations who bid for the right to represent them. If not for corporate relocation, the Indianapolis real estate market would be lifeless during the winter. Indianapolis had predictable seasons for real estate sales and the months of December, January and February were usually the doldrums. Miles looked out the window onto Mass Avenue as a light snow fell.

He thought about how the time seemed to go so quickly and on days like this, they hardly ever seemed to end.

The new concept now offered by Clear Choice Realtors was unique and Miles felt obligated to spread the good word, not only to the general public, but he also felt that his own colleagues and others who worked in the real estate industry should and would embrace the new concept.

From this thought Miles decided to call the Indianapolis Board of Realtors to speak with the professional standards director, Dottie Fuller. She was the person in charge of business ethics and other issues related to the conduct of the nearly 5000 member agents who practiced real estate sales within the central area of Indiana.

Miles didn't necessarily have an agenda, but he felt the need to discuss his business model with the director to see her take on the concept. After all, his idea was an ethical improvement over the current process. He expected some positive support. At least, that's what he thought.

Miles dialed the local number, "Board of Realtors," the voice on the other end of the line said.

"Dottie Fuller, please," Miles said.

"One moment, please," the voice said.

"Hello, this is Dottie."

"Hi Dottie, this is Miles Vincent," Miles said. The two had met numerous times. Miles had always been active with the local Board and during his years at Trinity he logged in plenty of time in meetings, committees and other work.

"Oh hi, Miles," Dottie replied, "how are things going for you these days?" she asked.

"Just fine, thanks," Miles said.

"How's business at Trinity?" Dottie asked.

"Oh…," Miles said with a slight pause, "I left Trinity a couple months ago to go out on my own and start a new company."

"That's great Miles!" Dottie said. "That takes some initiative to do that."

"Yes Dottie, I had thought about it for a while. I believe I have a new concept that you might be interested in knowing about, especially since the concept strengthens the agency relationship between agents and clients," Miles stated.

"Oh, really," Dottie said inquisitively, "and how might that work?"

"I came up with an idea last year and I am really excited about getting the word out about it and I thought you would be one who would like what I'm doing. I created a concept that eliminates limited agency," Miles said.

Dottie's immediate thought went to some other local agents who had become independent and eliminated limited agency by working solely as buyers' agents. There were some agents who preferred single agency: choosing to work exclusively for buyers, or those who chose to work exclusively for sellers. Although they were sparse in numbers in the Indianapolis area, most had arrived at the decision as a means to eliminate limited agency and the potential conflict of interest that could arise from it.

"So have you become an exclusive listing agent, Miles?" Dottie asked.

"Not exactly, Dottie," Miles explained. "I came up with a new concept where I can work with both buyers and sellers."

"And how is that?" Dottie asked, with some intrigue in her voice.

"I still work for buyers as a regular agent and guarantee them exclusive agency since I don't list homes any more. The new concept is for sellers. I no longer list homes, but instead, I function as a consultant to help sellers hire another agent. I avoid agency issues with the seller because my work is performed before the agency relationship is formed," Miles explained.

"Hmm, that's interesting Miles," Dottie said. "But how is it that you avoid the agency relationship with the seller?"

"Because the State of Indiana says that the agency relationship is formed between the listing agent and the seller at the moment when the listing contract is signed and I perform my services prior to any listing contract being signed," Miles said. "And that keeps me from having any chance of representing the buyer and seller in the same transaction.

"That's clever!" Dottie exclaimed.

"Well, clever or not, I did it because it's the right thing to do," Miles said. "I decided to make a stand against the unfairness, I mean, *possible unfairness* of limited agency, you know what I mean?" asked Miles.

"I don't know if it's a real problem, Miles. There are disclosures that protect both consumers and realtors if that situation arises. We really don't get that many complaints about it," Dottie stated.

"You might be right, Dottie, but I am talking about when it does arise. Do you think the disclosures are enough to protect consumers?"

"We follow the same policies that the National Association of Realtors and the Indiana Realtors Association follow, and I think that is sufficient," Dottie said with a tinge of admonition. She knew where Miles was heading with the discussion.

"Well Dottie, we have been using those same disclosures for years, but I want to ask you specifically about the conflict of interest that can arise during limited agency. For example, if a limited agent makes his proper disclosures to both the buyer and seller, is there any concern about the potential injustice that arises because the agent is compromised during the process?" Miles asked, and continued. "Hypothetically, don't you think we should step up to the plate and proactively do something to eliminate it?"

There was a brief silence at the other end. Dottie was aware of the inherent conflict, but it was inconceivable to imagine an overhaul of the current practice; this was something to be left alone even though Miles might be right. She became more calculated, even terse. "The policies and procedures are regularly reviewed and at this time there is little concern for issues that are backed locally, state-wide, and at the national level," she stated.

"Yes, but I am talking about the fact that if a limited agency transaction puts any consumer at a disadvantage, should we acknowledge it and do something to fix it?" Miles asked.

"I believe I answered that already, Miles," Dottie said, "and I am sorry I've got to cut this short because I have a meeting in a few minutes."

Miles knew she didn't have a meeting but what she said and how she said it confirmed the obvious: she wasn't interested in talking about it, much less doing anything about it.

"One last thing, Dottie," Miles said. "Business ethics in real estate pretty much is defined from a moral perspective on what we collectively believe is right or wrong, isn't that right?"

"I really have to go Miles," Dottie countered, deliberately not answering the question. "Good luck with your new business!" And then she hung up.

Miles sat in his office in mild disbelief, staring at the dial tone.

Mahi-Mahi

February 21, 2008

In nearly 10 years of selling real estate, Miles Vincent had served a number of buyers and sellers. He had always been conscientious about doing a good job for his clients so there was a natural referral network from the people who had used Miles as a real estate agent in the past. This is how he met Joe Vale, a professional photographer.

Miles was in his office on a Thursday morning. It was rainy, overcast and cool when his phone rang shortly after 9 am.

"Clear Choice Realtors," Miles answered.

"Good morning, this is Joe Vale and I got your name from a friend of mine. I want to sell my house this spring and he said you were a good person to talk to. He said you were doing a new way of selling, but I wasn't sure exactly what he meant."

"Thanks for calling, Joe," Miles began. "The service I offer helps you to hire another agent to list your home. It won't cost you a penny for my services and there's a good chance I will help you save money in the process."

Joe asked, "Now how are you going to save me money, Miles?"

"What's the most important thing when it comes to selling your home, Joe?" Miles asked

"I guess that would be maximizing the profit from the sale of my home," Joe replied.

"That's a great answer, Joe. I think you and most sellers would agree that getting the most profit out of your home ranks pretty high on the priority list.

The way I help you do that is to make the commission rate competitive among the agents you choose who will vie to list your home," Miles said.

"You mean it's not seven percent?" Joe asked.

"The State of Indiana, as well as most other states, makes it a law that real estate brokerages are not allowed to fix a commission rate. And that stems from anti-trust violation law which is federal. So it's negotiable. Part of my service is that I help negotiate the best rate we can get. You mentioned seven percent, but if I can get it down to six, then that would save you one percent. If you have a $200,000 home, that one percent means you saved $2000," Miles explained. "That's more money in your pocket!"

"Very cool!" exclaimed Joe. "This sounds interesting. But how are you paid?" he asked.

"I am paid a referral fee from the broker who earns your listing. And that is inclusive in your cost, so essentially, my service to you is free, Joe," Miles said.

"I understand now," said Joe. "When can we get started?"

"How about next Monday?" Joe asked.

"I think that will be fine," Miles said. He looked at his calendar and saw that he had no appointments in the morning. "Would 9 o'clock at my office be ok?" asked Miles.

"See you at nine," Joe replied.

"Thanks for the opportunity to help you, Joe," Miles said.

"No problem, Miles. I look forward to meeting you," Joe replied.

"Goodbye, Joe," said Miles.

Miles hung up the phone and rolled his chair back, interlocked his fingers behind his head and stretched. He was feeling good about things. He thought back to his days in Port Aransas and soon he imagined the boat the Hampton family chartered back in the summer of 1980. The family was local and they owned the old Tarpon Inn and Restaurant. The Tarpon Inn was the oldest existing business on the island. The hotel was built in the 1890s – a long, white, two-story building with a wide porch that looked east toward the Port Aransas harbor.

At one time near the turn of the century, Theodore Roosevelt had come to Port Aransas to fish for the renowned tarpon. Back in those days Port Aransas was teeming with tarpon in the bays and estuaries. The huge game fish were part of the legend and mystique of the island. How many great fishing stories were made up on the steps of the Tarpon Inn is a subject still under debate among the locals in Port Aransas.

The actual Tarpon Inn Restaurant was behind the hotel in a quiet, palm shrouded courtyard. It had a reputation for serving exquisite seafood, made by a revolving door of chefs who worked various tenures over the years. The Hampton family had owned and run the restaurant since anyone could remember, and as locals they had sea legs that would accommodate even the roughest of conditions, business or weather-wise.

But on this summer day the owner of the Tarpon Inn and Restaurant, William Hampton, was taking his wife and two children out for a day of deep sea fishing. Miles had all the poles, tackle and bait organized and ready to go and the charter boat was idling out in the ocean about 20 miles off shore. The captain was on board and so was another deckhand. It was a handy crew.

They had been out for nearly three hours and had seen nothing. The Gulf was calm and the charter boat rocked gently on the emerald colored water. They heard a screech overhead and everyone looked up to see a solitary gull float by. There were no clouds in the sky and the heat was beginning to stifle. The kids were in the air conditioned cabin playing games on a table that was bolted to the floor and had a lip around the edge to keeps things from scooting off when the seas got rough. The men were outside looking for anything.

"Shit, ain't nothing," cried Eddie, the other deckhand working the trip with Miles.

"No kidding, Eddie," Miles said.

"At least we have a beautiful day," said William Hampton. "It could have been storming or the seas could be high. If it's too rough the kids get sick sometimes."

"We got Dramamine and extra patches below," Miles said.

Everything was still and the boat creaked. The air was heavy with a palpable saltiness. Then Eddie pointed over the port stern, "There's a two-by-four floating over there, 'bout sixty yards." It was the first thing they had seen all day.

The captain yelled from the bridge, "We'll head over and look. It's pretty bright out and there might be some fish looking for some shade." The captain swung the boat around and passed within 20 yards on the lee side. Miles and Eddie had already prepared two poles, one with ribbon fish as bait, and the other pole was baited with hooties, small miniature mop-like lures that look exactly like a stringy mop with a hook embedded in the middle.

As they trolled by, a fish hit the bait. Miles handed the pole over to Mr. Hampton. A slight tug and the fish was hooked. They rushed to the side to see a mahi-mahi break the surface. The colorful blue and green fish was bright yellow underneath. The color was electric once you pulled them out of the water.

Then the captain yelled below, "I think there's a school of Dorado staying under that piece of wood."

Miles and Eddie quickly prepared the poles with hooties, sometimes putting three or four to a leader. By the next pass, they had four poles in the water. The kids came out and the fishing began. The next pass had more action as three of the lines were hit. Mr. Hampton pulled in two fish. Then Mrs. Hampton pulled in one. The fish were flopping on the deck in color spasms. Miles and Eddie tended to the harvest, getting them off the hooks and into the coolers.

They swerved and prepared for another pass. The four lines were in and loaded with hooties. This time all four rods bent.

"My gosh," said Luke, the Hampton's seven year-old son, "there's hundreds of 'em!"

In the next 45 minutes they caught 57 mahi-mahis. The coolers were full and Miles and Eddie began cleaning the fish. It didn't take long to clean a fish that had no scales and weighed between three and five pounds. They had all the fish filleted in less than an hour. All those fish fillets, as fresh as you could get it, cleaned and iced down.

It wasn't even noon and they had a boat full of fish. The captain was on the bridge when Mr. Hampton yelled, "Captain, I think we can head back to port. We have enough and we could get this fresh catch back to the restaurant."

"Aye, aye!" yelled the captain as he steered the boat back toward Port Aransas.

After the cleaning up had been done and everything was in its proper place, the Captain called everyone to the deck.

Miles flipped open one of the seat cushions on the starboard side and reached in for an armful of ice-cold Lone Star beer. He handed them out to everyone on the deck. They popped the tops and raised their cans.

"To a great morning of fishing!" said Eddie. "To the fish gods!" said Mr. Hampton. "Let's head back to port. We'll get these fresh fish into the chef. Everybody on the boat is invited to dinner at the Tarpon tonight!"

With that announcement, they headed north toward the Texas coast.

That evening, everyone showed up at the restaurant for a raucous celebration. The party sat in the Captain's Cove, a private dining room in which hung a huge blue marlin caught by Mr. Hampton when he was a boy: a 788 pound trophy fish.

They had fresh oysters, stone crab claws, 10-count shrimp as well as the fresh mahi-mahi, which was served with the usual homemade rolls, dirty rice and lots of beverages.

The phone rang and snapped Miles out of his Gulf daydream.

"Clear Choice Realtors," he said, "this is Miles Vincent speaking."

The Concept Introduction

March 5, 2008

The Indianapolis Board of Realtors had nearly 5000 member agents in central Indiana in 2008. The downtown area of Indianapolis had its own small chapter that held meetings on the first Wednesday of each month. Attendance at the meeting was sporadic, and when agents were busy, they tended to blow it off. When it was slow, the meetings were usually packed.

The market was beginning to heat up. Midwestern cities seemed to have cyclical markets for real estate and Indianapolis was no exception.

Miles was neatly dressed in a suit when he attended the March meeting. There were only about 30 agents who made the meeting, but Miles thought this would be a good place to get the word out about his concept. It was 11 am and the meeting was held at the Elbow Room, a downtown restaurant that had an upstairs banquet room.

Miles sat at one of the tables with a couple other agents from different companies. He glanced around the room and saw a handful of Trinity agents who were new to the downtown scene. Having them in the room made Miles a little anxious. The other Trinity agents knew who he was, but then, so did most of the other agents.

Everyone was eating before the meeting began and Miles looked at the meeting agenda.

The speaker was one of the city's deputy mayors. Miles was reading the agenda when a feedback screech from the podium shocked the room. The chapter president was trying to adjust the microphone.

"Sorry everybody," said Bill Barry, the chapter president. "Guess I hit the wrong button!" Although the banquet room was fairly large, it wasn't necessary to have a loudspeaker system. But they did it anyway so those people speaking looked professional and sounded louder than they normally would.

"I'd like to welcome everyone to this month's meeting," said Bill. "Looks like we have a good crowd today. Is the market heating up for everybody? Yeah!" He was trying to pump up the crowd. "Is anyone making any money?" The room was basically silent, but there were a couple of negative responses from new agents who weren't making any money.

"Before we get into today's meeting, we'll start with the roll call," Bill said. Roll call was done right after lunch and before the actual meeting began. Table by table, each agent stood up and announced who they were and who they worked for. It was also a moment for the agent to make a short announcement about anything, such as a new listing, or maybe a buyer who was looking for a particular property. They could have used the loudspeaker at the podium, but it wasn't necessary.

Miles had come today to announce his new office location and give a short description about his new idea. He thought the local chapter would be a good place to test his new idea; to see what kind of reaction he would elicit from the agents he worked with on a regular basis. It came to his turn, Miles stood up.

"Hello everybody. My name is Miles Vincent and most of you remember me working for Trinity, but I am now an independent broker working for my own company, Clear Choice Realtors." Miles was a little nervous and didn't want to take too much time. "I have developed a new concept I am excited to share with you fellow agents. I am now offering a new real estate concept that eliminates limited agency." The room was silent. Miles felt like he was standing on the high dive, like a seven year old jumping for the first time – petrified. "We still work with buyers in the traditional way of buyer representation, but the new concept is for sellers." Miles waited a moment and noticed that people were actually listening to him. "We no longer list properties, but rather, we work as a consultant for the sellers, helping them to hire another agent, such as yourselves, to list the property." Miles looked to blank stares. He was

The Fishy Side of Real Estate

about to sit down, but then realized he had forgotten to mention the new office location. "Oh, and we have opened a new office location in the 500 block of Mass Avenue."

Then a small giggle rustled at the back. It was another agent who had leaned over to whisper to another. Half the room heard the comment from the whisperer: "What idiot would give up half their business for a new idea?!"

Miles didn't hear the comment, but he quickly concluded his floor time with: "It would be great if I could give each one of you a referral this year!" Miles said with mustered enthusiasm. And then he sat down.

Gulliver's Travels

March 12, 2008

Paula and Bob Goldberg were not from Indianapolis, but like many professionals, a job had brought them there. Bob worked as an engineer for a large pharmaceutical firm in town and Paula worked for an accounting firm as an executive. They had two lovely girls, Alexandra and Katrina, who were nine and twelve years old.

The Goldbergs had lived in the southern suburbs for ten years and were ready to move to the city. They sent their girls to private school and they both commuted. They practically lived their lives in the city only to spend hours every week shuffling back and forth. Besides, the girls were older now and the city offered much more to do than the sleepy, conservative community where they were living now.

Bob's company was large enough that it had an in-house relocation service. Large companies often provide moving services for certain employees. The Goldbergs were relocating locally and the company had an incentive program that was convenient. Bob had inquired at HR for the specifics of the relocation program and was close to listing his home when he overheard a conversation in the company cafeteria. Two of his colleagues were discussing a new idea they had heard about real estate consulting. He heard one of them say, "the service doesn't cost anything to get the real estate advice and it can save you money at the same time."

Bob leaned over and interrupted, "Excuse me, but we're thinking about relocating to the city and I wouldn't mind checking out what you're talking about. Is that a company here in Indy?" Bob asked.

"Yeah, I saw it down on Mass Ave. It's a small real estate office called Clear Choice Realtors. There's a better explanation on the web," said the colleague.

"Hey, thanks," said Bob.

When Bob returned to his desk he googled 'clear choice realtors' and got a web address: www.ccrealtors.net. He clicked onto the site and read the page:

'Clear Choice Realtors will not list your home for sale, but will find someone who is qualified to do so…' Hmm. Bob thought to himself. Then he clicked on the mail button to Clear Choice Realtors and he wrote:

'Good afternoon. Interested in moving and have a house to sell. Find your idea interesting. Regards, Bob Goldberg.'

He hit the send button.

Miles heard the mail sound on his in-box as he was working on an advertisement. He turned to the keyboard and clicked on his in-box. He read the message and then answered back:

'Thanks for the inquiry. Happy to meet with you personally, to see if we can work together. Miles Vincent, Broker.'

Miles had enough experience to know that leads from the internet didn't always pan out. There was some strange, digital barrier that exists between people who meet on-line. The only way for an agent and a client to evaluate one another – to get the sense of trust necessary to work together – was to meet in the flesh.

Bob Goldberg was at his desk when his in-box beeped. He saw it was from Clear Choice Realtors. Bob wrote back: 'Can we meet tomorrow at St. Elmo's? I will bring my wife Paula along. 5:30 at the bar?'

Miles was looking at the computer screen when the in-box beeped. Miles wrote back: 'Looking forward to seeing you at St. Elmo's tomorrow at 5:30.'

'See you then,' was the immediate reply from Bob.

o o o

The next day Miles was busy showing houses all day with an out-of town client from South Carolina who was moving to Indianapolis. They had seen eleven different homes in four hours. Miles was taking him back to the hotel. It was

3:30 p.m. in the afternoon as Miles pulled in to the front entrance of the Westin Hotel. Miles pulled into a temporary parking space.

"We got a lot accomplished, Jim," Miles said. Jim Starr was the transfer who was referred to him by a former client.

"Yeah, that was great," Jim said, with a noticeable southern accent.

"Did you think any of those places looked worthy?" Miles asked.

"Wasn't wowed by anything, to tell you the truth," Jim replied.

"Finding the right place takes time," Miles said. "We will go in as many places as you need to make a good decision. And it's ok to be picky." Miles was thumbing through the stapled pages of places they had seen. After all, looking at eleven places in one day can be a dizzying exercise. After a while, all the facts and places and images begin to blend together and it's hard for anybody to keep all the details from each place separated.

Jim pointed to the listing Miles was looking at. "I did like that place, but the location was too close to the interstate."

Miles looked at the sheet and said, "We still plan on going out tomorrow. Would you like to see this one again?" Miles asked.

"Why not!" Jim laughed. "I only have a few days before I have to go back to Charleston."

"It's tough to look for a home when you are limited on time," Miles said. "We will get out as much as we can while you're here. Tomorrow we'll look at those places on the north side and see how you like those, ok?"

"Sounds great, Miles. See you tomorrow at nine," Jim replied as he swung open the passenger door.

"I'll send you those listings via email when I get back," Miles said.

Miles looked at the clock. It was 3:38 p.m. He needed to get back to the office to do some things before the 5:30 p.m. meeting at St. Elmo's.

It was a few minutes before the meeting when Miles walked into St. Elmo's. The bar was empty except for two businessmen. Miles carried only his business cards since he never went to an initial meeting with much paperwork; this was a time to meet the client and for the client to meet him. Miles thought it was a cleaner beginning, to focus 100% on the person in front and not encumber the meeting with anything extra. Miles reached in his shirt pocket to make sure he had put a few fresh business cards there, although he knew he had. Only once had he ever had to write his name on a napkin and he was so embarrassed, that he swore he would never go out in public without a business card in his pocket.

Miles had not yet taken a seat when he noticed a tall couple walk through the front door. The man had a look that Miles recognized: that expectant look, like someone searching for someone. That was the only clue Miles needed. He knew it was Paula and Bob Goldberg.

Within moments Miles covered the distance to the entryway. When their eyes met, the recognition was confirmed. Miles stuck out his hand. "You must be Bob and Paula," he said.

Bob returned the handshake. "Nice to meet you, Miles," Bob said

Miles turned to Paula, "It's a pleasure to meet you, Paula."

"Thanks for meeting us on short notice," Paula said.

"Would you like a table or should we sit at the bar?" asked Miles.

Bob pointed over to a small bar table against the wall with three empty chairs. "Let's sit right there."

They took their places and a waiter approached. Paula ordered a glass of wine while Miles and Bob ordered draft beer.

"Miles," Bob began, "I was at lunch and overheard a couple of coworkers discuss your new real estate service and I was... I mean, we were intrigued with your idea of a consulting service, and we would like to find out more about it."

"Thanks so much for the opportunity," Miles said. "The service I provide for sellers is novel. Essentially, I am going to help you hire another real estate agent to list your home." Miles paused for a moment to see if there was recognition on Bob and Paula's faces. 'Somewhat blank,' he thought to himself.

Then Paula spoke. "Miles, to be honest, we have been thinking about moving to the city for some time and we have talked with Bob's HR department about the relocation package they offer employees. It has some pretty decent incentives should we elect to choose that service."

Then Bob interrupted, "But we haven't signed anything yet and we wanted to explore all the options available to us."

Miles was thinking. He heard Paula and wondered if they had already made up their mind. "Let me say that my service is of no cost to you, and there's a chance I could put more money back into your pocket." Miles asked, "Isn't your goal to maximize the profit on the sale of your home?"

"Absolutely," Bob said, "that is at the top of our list."

"Bob," Paula said to her husband, "did you tell Miles that we have already spoken with the relocation agent that HR recommended?"

Miles felt his heart sink. He felt he was losing ground while the waiter approached and served the drinks. Miles stared at the draft beer for a moment watching the bubbles rise, grasping for direction.

"Although my service is new, one of the great things for sellers is that the top agents are identified in their specific area of residence. If your home is in Greenwood, then we are going to focus on the agents who are producing sales in your specific area," Miles said and he had their attention now. "Remember that book Gulliver's Travels?" he said out of the blue.

"Sure," said Paula, "William Dafoe wrote that classic."

"Well there's a line from that book that says: 'Nothing is great nor small, unless by comparison.'" Now Miles saw some light, like a dark room that is suddenly illuminated by an open door. "That is a classic line from a great book, but my point is that if you have only spoken to one agent, maybe it might make sense to talk to a couple more. We can compare them. Let me offer this: I will produce the agent statistics from your area, then I will also provide the production specific to the agent which your relocation department recommended. If you decide that you still want to use your company relocation service, then I will back out like I never existed. It will not cost you a penny for my service, whether you work with me or not."

"There's no harm in getting information," Bob said. "And we don't know much about the referral agent yet, I have only spoken to him on the phone a couple times."

"That's fair," said Paula. "We don't know much about the company's referral, we just assumed they get the best agents to work for us."

Miles was excited. "To make it easy for both of you, why don't I drive out to your place in the next week or two. I'll bring the agent statistics relative to your area, then I'll bring the stats on your referral agent. Then you can decide what direction you want to go, does that sound fair?"

Paula and Bob looked at each other, then at Miles. They were fine with that. "Like I said," Bob replied, "there's no harm in getting information. Miles, we're out of town next week so maybe we could schedule this meeting for the third week in March. How about the 22nd? That's a Saturday. Will that work?"

"That will be fine on the 22nd. And by the way," added Miles, "what is the name of the agent that Relocation referred to you, Bob?"

"His name is Buddy Frank," answered Bob. "He works for Trinity Realtors."

Miles eyebrows went north. 'This will be interesting,' he thought to himself.

Networking the Idea

March 17, 2008

Miles was in his office on a Monday morning with a cup of coffee and 45 minutes of time. A new buyer was meeting him at the small office on Mass Avenue. They were going to see five homes, all in the downtown area, just minutes apart from one another.

He had been thinking about target markets for his idea. He felt strongly about the fact that he could promise buyers 100% allegiance without any compromising. There would be no diluting of his agency duties to the buyer. He knew there was an ethical advantage to the concept. 'It guarantees buyers that the agent will never compromise his ability to represent them,' he thought. 'The added layer of protection for buyers may appeal to mortgage companies and their buying clients.' His heart quickened with excitement as he thought about the potential.

He picked up his phone and punched the directory for Nicole Hanks, a former agent for Trinity who had gone into the mortgage business several years ago. She was hired by a small, local bank that added mortgage services. Within two years she had become VP of the mortgage division. Miles had met Nicole before. They had been on opposite sides of a transaction on a home in Zionsville several years ago. Miles recalled the transaction as uneventful and having no problems. He had even had some closings using the Community Bank mortgage department. 'Maybe the new idea would appeal to a small lender,' he thought.

Miles dialed her office number.

"Community Bank, may I help you?" said the voice at the end of the line.

"Nicole Hanks, is she available?" Miles asked.

"May I ask who's calling, please?"

"This is Miles Vincent."

"One moment please."

Miles sat in anticipation when a voice came through.

"Hello Miles, this is Nicole. How are you doing?"

"Fine, thanks, Nicole. Do you have a couple minutes?" asked Miles.

"Sure, but I have a meeting in 15 minutes, if it doesn't take that long," Nicole answered.

Community Bank had grown much larger over the past several years. They were hiring loan officers every month. Nicole's meeting involved the hiring of a new employee.

Miles spent the next few minutes explaining the concept to Nicole. When Miles waxed about his displeasure with the conflict of interest that can arise during limited agency, it struck a nerve with Nicole. She had been dissatisfied with several agents who had performed such a transaction with her clients. There were several incidents recently that were swimming inside her head. Nicole held an Indiana real estate broker's license and was aware of the limitations, and the possible conflict of interest associated with limited agency. There were two recent transactions in particular where the buyers had complained to a loan officer about the agent in the deal who had represented both the buyer and seller. As well, she had to assuage a couple last week whose dissatisfaction with a limited agency transaction, and the inability of staff to adequately explain the dilemma, had eventually gotten to her desk and left her to explain the problem. She recalled the conversation succinctly. She had not liked that situation and Miles new concept had her wheels turning.

"That's really interesting, Miles," Nicole said. "I like what you're doing. I recently had a conversation with some clients who felt they were shortchanged during the transaction. I really like your idea about promising buyers 100% agency."

"I truly believe that buyers benefit from an agent who represents only them and no one else," Miles added. "Buyers have a guarantee that they will be fully represented without any chance of limited agency entering the picture. Nicole, do you think that's worth anything?"

A moment passed before Nicole spoke. She was thinking about how many complaints had come in from loan officers over the past year. "Yes, Miles, you make a clear point. I'd like to present the idea internally. Why don't you give me a couple weeks, Miles. I'll get back in touch with you after I talk to some people."

"That sounds great, Nicole," Miles said. He thought about how many agents he would need if the idea really caught on. "I look forward to hearing from you."

"Thanks for calling, Miles. I really like what you are doing. Have a great week," she added.

"You too, Nicole. Thanks for your time. Bye now."

Miles hung up the phone excited with the idea that he could get referrals directly from a lending institution. He glanced at his watch. He still had some time before his client arrived. He turned to the computer and clicked on his e-mail to send a new message. He typed in 'pau' and the name of Paulson came to the screen. He clicked on the name and sent Gary Paulson a message.

Dear Gary,

Hope things are going well. You know I started my own office using the concept I talked with you about last summer. Let me know when you have a few minutes. Maybe we could meet at Starbucks for a coffee in the next week or so.

Miles Vincent, Broker
Clear Choice Realtors

He hit the send button.

Miles looked at the time. He still had twenty minutes until his buyer showed up. He looked at his schedule and saw the Saturday meeting with the Goldberg family. He hadn't done anything yet to run the statistics for the Greenwood area.

Miles turned to the computer and clicked on the 'RealServe' icon. He logged in and went to the member section and keyed in the last name 'Frank'. Four 'Franks' appeared on the screen. Miles clicked on "Buddy Frank" and saw the agent number assigned to Buddy from the local board. He went to another screen to search Buddy Frank's production, all his listings, and sales that he transacted in the past two years.

Miles hit the search button. There on the screen in front of him was the actual production of the referring agent that Bob Goldberg's company had recommended. He looked it over carefully. Miles perused the transactions: 37 closed transactions, ten active listings, twenty expired listings, two pending transactions. Miles narrowed the search down to the 37 closed transactions. He looked at the areas where Buddy Frank had been doing business. The closed transactions occurred north in Fishers, Carmel and Anderson. These were north side communities that were 30 to 40 miles away from where Bob and Paula Goldberg lived! Miles was shocked that the referral would go to someone who had no experience in a specific area. 'Why would the company do that?' Miles asked himself. Then, as quickly as the question entered his mind, the answer followed nearly as quick – 'the money.'

Miles went back to the summary production screen and printed off Buddy Frank's real estate stats. Then he stuck them in the Goldberg file for Saturday's meeting.

Corporate Greed

March 24, 2008

Miles was in his car heading south to Greenwood for his 10 am appointment with Paula and Bob Goldberg. He had the CD player blasting the Dire Straits second album as he merged onto the downtown, I-65 ramp.

He sticks to his guns
Takes the road as it comes
It takes the shine off his shoes

Says it a shame
You know it may be a game
But I won't play to lose

Miles listened closely to the lyrics. He thought Mark Knopfler was the English Bob Dylan and a better guitar player to boot. Knopfler had a unique finger style technique when he played and could make that Stratocaster sing.

And she tells him that he's crazy
And she's saying listen baby
I'm your wife

And she tells him that he's crazy
For gamblin' with his life

But he climbs on his horse
You know he feels no remorse
He just kicks it alive

Miles glanced at the folder on the passenger seat. It had Goldberg written on the tab. Inside the folder were the production figures for the Goldberg property. Miles could hardly wait to show Bob and Paula the agent production stats. He imagined what their response would be when he showed Buddy Frank's stats: the fact that he had had no experience in Greenwood smelled fishy.

Twenty minutes later Miles pulled into Cherry Creek Hills, the Goldberg's subdivision in suburban Greenwood. He looked at the homes which were built three to four years ago. '350 to 500 thousand for this,' Miles thought to himself. There were only about five different styles in the 200-home neighborhood: all the homes looked the same. 'Without numbered addresses, how could you find anyone in this neighborhood?' Miles thought.

But Miles did find the Goldberg's home without a problem, since the GPS lady told him where to go at each turn. "Turn left at the next intersection," the female robot-voice said on the phone speaker.

Bob was in the front yard when Miles pulled into the driveway. Bob waved. Miles waved back.

Bob approached the car as Miles got out with his file folder.

"Good to see you, Miles," Bob said.

They shook hands.

"Nice to see you again, Bob," Miles said.

"Let's go inside," Bob said as he motioned toward the front door. They walked in the clean, bright foyer and the girls ran screaming into another room.

"Girls, let's hold off on the chasing for a while," Bob instructed the breathless sisters who were laying on the floor in the living room.

Paula walked into the foyer and greeted Miles.

"Hello, Miles" Paula said. She reached out to shake his hand. "Please, come into the kitchen. Coffee?"

"Please. Cream, too," Miles said.

Miles and Bob sat down while Paula poured a cup of coffee for Miles.

"Thanks for having me down today," Miles began, "I guess we can get started with the statistics for home sales in your area."

Miles had produced three identical sets of stats for the Goldbergs. For the next twenty minutes he explained broker production and specific agent production over the last two years. The sales were specific to like subdivisions in the Greenwood area which were similar to the Goldberg's home. About four brokers dominated the sales in the $400K to $650K range. There were about nine agents who had more production than the others. Eight of those agents worked for one of the four brokers. The other lone producer was a small independent broker. The Indianapolis market was dominated by the large national firms and only a handful of smaller, independent brokers ever grew large enough to be competitive.

"That's interesting," said Paula, "that most of the sales are done by franchises, except for Davis Realty."

"That's what I usually find," Miles said "that the big firms dominate the market. It's the same reason McDonalds and Burger King do so well in Indianapolis!" Miles was joking, but it was true: Hoosiers were cautious about start-ups and felt comfortably numb plying the old standards like White Castle or Denny's. Real Estate was the same: many people felt an agent affiliated with a national franchise meant they were getting experience and quality service. Agents making their own way as independents were automatically viewed with skepticism or even disdain. Much like a non-chain restaurant, working with a non-chain real estate agent meant an additional layer of consumer scrutiny; as though a tacky jacket with an embroidered logo makes somebody a good agent.

"Paula, I truly believe that you and Bob have the best chance to sell your house by employing those agents who are doing the most business in your area," Miles said. "As you can see, there are a number of top-producers in your price range and area who stand out." Miles pointed to the page where the agent statistics were compared line by line. "Look at that: two agents from the same office having lots of sales in four subdivisions similar to yours. But look at the average Days on Market – these agents took considerably longer to sell homes, on the average," he said pointing to the statistics.

"Look at how many expired listings that agent had," said Bob pointing to a column.

"Yeah, looks like this guy really had a lot of listings that expired. The general public doesn't get to see this information," said Miles. "But I think the information helps sellers to find the most productive agents, and in turn, properties often sell faster. That's what I have been seeing for sellers who use this consulting concept."

"It will be interesting to see how the relocation referral stacks up. What's his name again, Bob?" Paula asked.

"Buddy Frank from Trinity Realtors," Bob replied.

Miles perked up, sensing the moment, he reached into the folder.

"Frankly, I just happened to bring in the stats on Buddy," Miles stated tongue in cheek. Paula laughed. Bob didn't.

Miles took out three copies of Buddy Frank's production and gave a copy to each. "Bob, I was wondering how your relocation department referred Buddy?" Miles asked. They all looked at the paper scrutinizing the listings and sales that Buddy had done in the last two years. Paula's eyes widened a bit. "I cannot believe that there is not one sale in our area! All his production is north, even as far up as Anderson. Why would they refer a realtor that has no experience in our area?" Paula asked incredulously.

"Unfortunately, it appears your relocation department is more interested in the relationship with the agent than they are about your welfare. I can tell you that this agent has no clue about schools, local contacts or the information that would help to sell your home. That's why I recommend dealing with the top producers in specific areas," Miles stated. "Your best chance to sell your home is by using those agents who are most familiar with the specifics of the home and area. That's what contributes to the expedient sale of a home."

"Dammit to hell," Bob said. He was agitated that Relocation would make such a poor referral choice. Obviously, the referral didn't have much to do with servicing its own employee. Bob thought that, but didn't say it.

"It's all about the money," Miles said.

"What do you think, Paula?" Bob asked his wife.

Paula didn't look too happy. "I think we should go forward with Miles and use his consulting services. After all, it doesn't cost anything to use the service and I am not happy about what we just found out," Paula said as she picked up

Buddy's production stats and held it up, pointing at it like she might shoot a nine millimeter bullet out her index finger.

Inside, Miles was smiling. He just landed another consulting job.

Get Rich Quick!

April 24 2008

Miles was in his office preparing for the day. The buyers market was in full bloom and everybody working in real estate was busy. Real estate was a great business to be in and there was no better time than spring. The wisteria blossoms were fragrant; the flowers were celebrating the new season with color. The leaves on the trees had the light green color that comes early in the season. The air was fresh.

Miles was looking over his calendar when he realized that it had been over a month since his discussion with Nicole Hanks, the VP of Community Bank Mortgage. He clicked on his e-mail and scrolled to 'Hanks' and sent this message:

'Nicole,

Hope things are going well for you in the mortgage business. Just following up from our conversation last month and wondering if you had made any progress with your inquiry.

Looking forward to hearing from you,

Miles Vincent

Broker, Clear Choice Realtors'

Then the phone rang. Miles picked it up after the first ring.

"Clear Choice Realtors, this is Miles speaking," he said.

"Hey Miles, it's been a while. This is Brad Western. I don't know if you remember me, but our kids go to school together," Brad said.

"Oh, sure Brad; nice to hear from you," Miles said. Thanks for calling. Anything I can help you with?"

"Not me personally," Brad said, "but I have some friends of mine that need some help."

"What kind of help do they need?" asked Miles.

"We have some friends who attended one of those real estate seminars. It seems like everyone's making a fortune in the real estate market these days, but they attended one of those seminars where they show you how to make quick money, you know, get rich quick," Brad said.

"Well, I don't know about 'quick money' but there's lots of opportunity out there," Miles said.

"Our friends – heck they're not even married yet – they bought five rental properties together and now they are kind of freaking out," Bob explained.

"Why are they freaking out?" asked Miles.

"They seem to be in over their heads and don't know what to do next," Brad said with remorse.

"Hmm. Well, Brad, where did they buy the rentals and how much did they pay for them?" Miles asked.

"Mostly they were duplexes on the east side, around the Brookside area. I think they paid 50 to 75 thousand for each, but they got a package loan to buy all of them and now they are scared they made a mistake," Brad said. "Do you have any advice to give them?"

"My advice would be to get busy and rent them out!" Miles said with emphasis.

"They said they all needed work," Brad said.

"And they paid that much for those properties in that area?" Miles remarked in a surprised tone. "Did they have an agent working for them?"

"I don't think so. They bought the properties as a package from an investor. I guess there were lots of them at the seminar," stated Brad.

"The best advice I can give is what I just said – get those places fixed up and rented out," Miles said flatly. "I'm surprised the lender approved that loan for those properties in that particular area, but lenders seem to approve everybody these days. I would also suggest they use an agent any time they consider buying property; looks like they jumped in without getting all the facts."

"Yeah, they're pretty bummed out about it," Brad remarked.

"I don't know what I can do to help them, but if they want to talk about it, have them give me a call," Miles said.

"Thanks for your time, Miles. I'll pass your name along to my friends and I'll tell them what you said," Brad replied.

"Sounds good, talk to you later, Brad," Miles said.

Miles hung up the phone and wondered how many people were sucked into those highly publicized seminars. Every week there seemed to be another full page ad in the paper announcing a new real estate guru who rode the frenzied tide of enthusiasm into some hotel where pie-eyed investors sat, listened, then swallowed the bait. Mortgage representatives were as common as piranhas in the Amazon. These real estate pitchmen had helped rocket the real estate market to new heights, which had a very positive effect on the lending industry.

On the back side of the real estate boom, Wall Street financiers had created a product tied to the higher interest rates associated with all those approved loans: a financial derivative product. It was a new product entirely and it was backed by all those risky deals. They were selling billions and everyone, including international governments, pension funds, speculators, investors and even grandma and grandpa couldn't refuse a fund that paid 15 to18 percent annually. This American-made investment attracted global attention and suckered the world into the alluring concept of easy money. But the Dow Industrial Average was over 13,000 in the last week of April, 2008 and business was going along just fine.

Miles remembered how he and his wife had saved money for almost two years before they bought their first house in the late 1980s: they had saved enough to put 20 percent down. Nobody did that anymore. Miles recalled many recent closings where buyers put no money down, and in some cases buyers walked away from the closing table with a check. Why would the lenders want all that risk?

It had to be the money. Except for their own greed, they loved easy money as much as they did anything.

Miles wondered if it was too good to be true. As long as he was closing deals, the money kept flowing.

Meeting the CEO

May 1, 2008

Miles was sitting at a Starbucks with a cup of coffee shortly before 11 am. The local Board was having a meeting downtown at noon, and he planned to go with his colleague, Gary Paulson. They had exchanged e-mails and were planning to go to the meeting together, but Miles was interested in getting Gary on board. He needed a couple more agents to spread the good word about the concept.

Out the window he saw Gary's car pull into the parking lot. He was driving a Jaguar. Miles watched him get out of the car. Miles got up to meet Gary at the door.

"Hey, Gary," Miles said, "thanks for meeting me this morning."

The two shook hands. "Nice to see you, Miles," Gary said.

Gary got a coffee and they sat at a comfortable sofa in the corner.

"So how are things going for you, Gary?" Miles asked.

"Really good at the moment," Gary replied. "And how about you, Miles, how's your new idea coming along?"

"Not bad, but it's been a little frustrating getting the concept out. Nobody seems to want to talk about it," Miles said, "but for the clients using the new consulting method, I would say it opens their eyes as far as the listing process goes. I am amazed how much sellers don't know and I think they appreciate the service. I never have an agenda, I'm just there as an advocate for the seller, trying to educate them so they make good decisions when selecting an agent."

"It's a neat concept, Miles." Gary said. "How's the response among agents you contact for the consulting?"

"At first, I thought they wouldn't do it, but I am extremely professional and complimentary about their work. They seemed to be a little surprised. I have to disclose that there are three agents competing for the listing, but they all seem to do it. Only a couple of agents have declined," Miles explained.

"If you think about it, Miles, why wouldn't an agent want a listing?" Gary asked, but it was more of a statement than a question.

"Maybe they have enough business and they don't want to fork out the referral fee," Miles said.

"I would do it if you called me," Gary stated.

"If your name comes up during the stat search, you'll know immediately!" Miles said happily. "But I never give any agent a referral unless they have the productivity to back it up in the area that is researched. That would bastardize the concept. I recently gave out a referral to an agent who worked in the same office as my cousin. When I made the initial call, this agent was shocked that I wouldn't give the referral to my cousin, whose office was next door to the referring agent!"

"Well, you know how referrals work most of the time, Miles," Gary said. "It's usually just a phone call."

"I explained to her that my cousin didn't have any production in the area I was researching. I explained that the consulting method identifies the top producers in a particular area, and that she was one of them. She still couldn't believe I wouldn't make the referral to my cousin," Miles stated.

"It's hard to break old habits," Gary said.

"Tell me about it! The culture of how we do business hasn't changed much for 50 years," Miles said.

"Don't you think the internet changed things?" Gary asked.

"The internet only made the availability of information easier for consumers; that's about it. In fact, the internet has been to the detriment of many home buyers," said Miles.

"Oh, come on, Miles, you cannot be serious about that," Gary said in disbelief.

"I'm not talking about the availability of information, I am talking about the fact that when a consumer uses the net for home searching, any inquiry about a property goes directly to the listing agent," Miles stated succinctly, "and that increases the likelihood of the listing agent representing the buyer."

"Wow, I guess you're right about that," Gary said, realizing Miles was right. "You make a good point."

"You know, Gary, it's not like listing agents refer their lead generation out to some other realtor," Miles said.

"You're right about that, Miles!" Gary replied.

"So Gary," Miles said, "what do you think about joining the company?"

Gary had a surprised look on his face. He wasn't expecting Miles to ask him that.

"Well, I'll have to think about it," Gary replied. "You know I usually list more than I sell, Miles."

"Then you'll be a natural at consulting!" Miles said happily.

"Yeah, but I have a lot of listings at the moment. But I do like the concept. It certainly is more straightforward for consumers," Gary replied.

"You don't have to answer right now, Gary. Think about it and we can talk later. Think we should head downtown to the meeting?" Miles asked.

"I have to cancel. Something came up that I have to do and I can't make it," Gary said.

"No problem, Gary. Think about what we talked about and we can get together later," Miles said.

They walked out of the Starbucks and headed to their cars. They waved at each other as Miles backed out and headed downtown.

When he arrived for the meeting, which was being held at the Scottish Rite Cathedral, Miles parked his car and headed for the door. Halfway across the parking lot, he saw the CEO of the local Indianapolis Real Estate Board, Sonny Scheizer. He was headed to the meeting as well. Sonny had been the CEO for over twenty years. He was a small man with watery eyes. He was wearing a custom-made Italian suit and carried a leather briefcase.

Miles approached him and said, "Hello Mr. Scheizer," Miles said as he reached out to shake his free hand, "I'm Miles Vincent."

"Pleased to meet you, Miles, anything I can help you with?" Sonny asked.

"No sir, I don't need any help, but I was wondering if I could get your opinion on something," Miles replied. They started walking toward the door.

The Fishy Side of Real Estate

"Sure," replied Sonny, "I'm always there for our agents; what's on your mind, Mr. Vincent?"

"I started a new business concept this year and I'd like your opinion on it," Miles stated.

"And what concept is that?" Sonny asked.

"I created a new method of transacting real estate that eliminates limited agency," Miles stated.

Sonny smiled and said, "Good for you, I wish you luck."

"I was more interested in your opinion on limited agency. Do you think we walk a thin line when an agent represents both the buyer and seller in the same transaction?" Miles had said it clearly. There was a moment of silence. Sonny didn't like the question.

"Well Mr. Vincent, the Indianapolis Board of Realtors is always concerned about how we perform in the marketplace, but we represent all member agents in central Indiana and limited agency is permissible provided the agent makes the proper disclosures," Sonny replied.

"You don't think the inherent conflict of interest is something we should be concerned about?" Miles asked pointedly.

"As long as the proper disclosures are made, I have no problem with it, Mr. Vincent," Sonny said.

They reached the door and Miles held it open.

"Nice talking with you, Mr. Vincent."

Miles was left holding the door as Sonny Scheizer walked down the steps of the Scottish Rite Cathedral and across the terrazzo floor to the meeting.

Addressing Issues
May 2, 2008

Miles was in his office the next morning thinking about his conversation with Sonny Scheizer. It was hard to understand why there was no more real conversation about the vagaries of limited agency, but then Miles thought that the local Board was interested in protecting the rights and livelihood of its members, not the general public. Still, the lack of compassion of addressing the limited agency issue, the fact that nobody wanted to discuss it, was bothering Miles.

He had been reading the local paper about an issue regarding the State Regulatory Commission. They had been reporting on unethical behavior at the highest level of state officials and a large utility company – they had been caught usurping their public obligations and now the newspaper was exposing their unethical behavior. Two attorneys representing the utility company had already been fired because of the scandal. Miles felt that the paper was doing the right thing in uncovering the misdeeds.

Miles thought there was an analogy between ethical inconsistencies. 'Maybe the Indianapolis Star would find the consulting concept interesting,' he wondered to himself.

Miles went to his computer and searched for the paper's website. He clicked on the business section, then scrolled down the side to find the business editor. He clicked on the business editor's name, Tom Shields, and sent this e-mail:

Dear Mr. Shields,

I have been following your story about ethical concerns with the public regulatory commission. Thanks for keeping an eye out for your readers' best interests. I'd like to bring attention to a new business concept that directly deals with a common conflict of interest that arises sometimes during real estate transactions: limited agency. Limited agency is where one agent represents both buyer and seller in the same transaction.

Earlier this year I started a company that eliminates that conflict and I was wondering if that might appeal to you for a business story in your newspaper. For more information on the concept please visit my website at www.ccrealtors.net. Looking forward to hearing from you.

Miles Vincent,
Broker, Clear Choice Realtors

Miles thought that any publicity would be good for business. He was optimistic that the paper would find his concept noteworthy. After all, weren't they interested in the best interests of their readers? Wouldn't a new real estate method that improved the agency relationship between the agent and the client be worthwhile to their readers? Even though Miles had been disappointed from the reaction of his peers, he thought this issue would surely stir the editorial staff at the local paper in a positive way.

'There's a first time for everything,' Miles thought to himself. Then he thought about the time he caught his first fish in Port Aransas.

It was during spring break from UT-Austin when Miles and his college buddies drove with the rest of the college buffalo herd to the Gulf of Mexico. Thousands of students converge along the Texas coast and Port Aransas is one of the top places to visit for spring break.

They had driven four hours from Austin to reach Aransas Pass. It's only a few miles from there to Port Aransas, and the only way to get to the island is by a state-run car ferry that holds about 20 vehicles. There were about five ferries in operation that crossed the channel, but the line of cars backing up was over a mile long. Cars, trucks and vans filled with inebriated college students waiting in line to cross the channel. It took almost two hours of waiting to get to the front of the line. By then, half the beer was gone.

They went directly to the beach where thousands of students were doing what most college students do: drink and get sunburned. The group Miles was with didn't even get a hotel room. They figured they could sleep on the beach, and if they needed restroom facilities, the county beach offered that.

The following day Miles was up earlier than his buddies. He had brought his fishing pole and wanted to go fishing. It was about a mile to the jetty which was built far out into the water. He took his tackle box and pole and started walking toward the jetty. Along the way he spotted a small, rusted-out girl's bicycle with a large basket on the front. It looked abandoned laying there in the sand. Miles propped it up, bounced it a couple times to get the sand off, and then tested the tires for air. It was ride-worthy! He put his tackle box in the basket, then held the pole in his left hand and pedaled off down the beach. Miles looked funny riding a bike that was too small for him. His knees were practically hitting his chest as he pedaled along, but it was faster than walking.

Minutes later he made it to the jetty and started riding that little bike seaward. About half way out he stopped to fish. There were dozens of people fishing, but Miles was the only one on a bike.

He got into his tackle box and assembled the rod and lure. Then he cast into the channel side of the jetty. Miles watched as a huge tanker passed by. All the ships that went into Corpus Christi had to pass through this channel. A huge shadow passed over Miles as the monster tanker cruised by without a sound.

Twenty minutes later Miles caught his first fish. He landed an eight-pound red drum, commonly called redfish, one of the best tasting fish in the Gulf. It wasn't much of a fight and Miles reeled the light red-colored fish to the rocks, grabbed the line, then stuck his fingers under the gill to hold it up. He was ecstatic and he didn't want to throw it back. He wanted to cook it for dinner and eat it with his friends.

So Miles decided to load up and head to the county beach fish cleaning station. He put the fish in the wire basket, then placed the tackle box on top of it, put the pole in his left hand, and pedaled off. Miles looked ridiculous riding that small bike down the jetty with the red drum in the basket. Another odd thing was that a flock of seagulls was following him overhead, screaming against the soft, buffeting wind, screaming at Miles.

The Fishy Side of Real Estate

The flock of seagulls followed him all the way to the fish-cleaning station. He got to the old wooden tables that had been there for years. He leaned the bike against the table, took out the tackle box and removed a long-bladed knife and put the red drum on the table.

Miles looked above him and saw the seagulls: they were screaming at him, hovering in place against the steady Gulf breeze. Miles knew they wanted part of that fish.

Miles set about cleaning the fish and took the fillet knife into the belly of the fish. He cut the fish under the throat and slit the fish open, running the blade back toward the tail. Fish guts oozed out. The seagulls multiplied in numbers, hovering and screaming overhead.

Miles used the fillet knife to cut the entrails into smaller pieces. Then he grabbed a piece and flung it up in the air. Seagulls frenzied themselves to jockey into position for the fresh morsels. They were fighting each other over the spoils. Miles was fascinated. He spent the next few minutes enjoying the spectacle, launching tidbits high into the air. Never once did any of the guts hit the ground. The gulls got every piece that was thrown skyward.

The phone rang. Miles snapped out of his daydream to answer the phone and grabbed it like a fish hitting the bait.

"Good morning, Clear Choice Realtors, Miles Vincent speaking, may I help you?" he asked.

Cross Country Encounter
October 4, 2008

The summer flew by, and then the fall arrived, bringing in the cooler air and shorter days. Miles had kept himself busy. Business had slowed down somewhat, but that was predictable at this time of year. The market, however, was having its problems, including the Dow Jones, which fell 2000 points from late September into early October. Markets were known to have corrections every so often, but this time it would not recover as quickly. The index averages started dropping like an iron anchor in deep water, but the anchor had a couple more months of dropping to do before it hit bottom.

Fall meant Miles got to spend more time with his two daughters, Valerie and Hanna. Valerie ran cross country in the fall and track in the spring. She went to a large public school that had a state caliber program for athletics. Valerie was pretty good and ran on the varsity cross country team. Miles didn't miss a meet. Dressed in a jogging suit, Miles was driving to see a large invitational meet where the competition would feature some of the best cross country teams in the state. The meet was being held at a north side course, twenty minutes by car from downtown.

Although things were ok with him and he was pleased at the initial public response to the Clear Choice consulting concept, Miles rued his lack of success and acceptance from his own peers. As he pulled onto College Avenue and drove north, Miles mulled over the things that had occurred during the last nine months. He was baffled and surprised by the responses from his own colleagues. He thought about Nicole Hanks and the fact that she never returned an e-mail or a phone call. How could someone be initially so positive about an idea, then suddenly act like you're not even there? His unanswered e-mail to the Indianapolis Star's Tom Shields. He had even spoken on the phone with Tom to talk to him about how the concept enhanced the agency duties owed to the client, but the business editor was slippery about his interest, let alone give an honest opinion on a new idea. After the rebuff, Miles wrote the Star's Chief Editor, Lynn Rucker, and posed the same ethical issue, pointing out the same injustices that can potentially infect a transaction. Miles commended the paper's coverage of the utility fiasco and felt his own concept was worthy of discussion. But not a word back. Like shouting into a canyon and not even hearing an echo. The Star showed no interest.

And his fruitless discussion with Sonny Scheizer in the parking lot got nothing accomplished. In fact, he knew he had been blown off. Miles remembered the small man going down the stairs in his nice suit. He was sitting comfortably at the helm of the local real estate ship and he really didn't have any incentive to change things. Agent membership was at an all time high and times were good, so why run the ship aground? Why complicate the public's understanding with an ethics issue? What would be the point of educating home buyers and sellers about a service that guarantees an upgraded agency relationship? Maybe the collective powers thought the information would disrupt everyone's way of doing business. Maybe it would be the equivalent of throwing a shoe into fresh seafood gumbo. Miles had followed up the bland parking lot discussion with an e-mail addressed to Sonny Scheizer. Miles wrote a more eloquent, stated approach to the matter, but even after several weeks, there was no answer from Sonny. Miles concluded correctly that Sonny didn't want to talk about it, in an e-mail, or otherwise.

Again, he remembered the fear of snorkeling in Grand Cayman, the black abyss. He was over a mysterious, unknown depth, and floating above it.

And now, his heart was pounding for another reason. Why wouldn't the rest of his colleagues stand up for what they knew was wrong?

He loathed that Dottie Fuller, the director of Professional Standards, did not want to discuss a dilemma that tempted many agents. Miles almost choked on the hypocrisy of a person whose job was to monitor ethics, then the refusal to even discuss it! It gnawed at him like sea worms slowing digesting the wooden hull of a sunken boat.

In the first year of doing the consulting work, Miles had become proficient at helping sellers save time and money. The consulting service was under the radar, but enough people were talking about it so that it kept him busy.

Miles' own understanding of real estate agency – specifically, the attributes: care – accountability – loyalty – obedience – and disclosure, owed to a client during the real estate transaction, had been honed. The consulting service had him listening to lots of good, professional agents making plausible listing presentations, so it was natural that the subject of agency would come up. It wasn't difficult for the subject to come up and when it did, Miles sat quietly in the chair next to the seller, ready to question, rather gladly, any situation where limited agency may rear its ugly head…'Even this year, how many listing agents had skated too far out onto the treacherous pond?' Miles thought to himself. He recalled one of the traps and played it out in his mind:

'So Mr. ReMax agent, could you please explain to my client exactly how your internal relocation department works? There's a clear advantage having a national franchise referring leads back to your central Indiana ReMax Office, but if those referrals go directly to you, wouldn't that set up a situation where you are representing the buyer and the seller in the same transaction?' The listing agents, once they skated onto the specifics of limited agency, often painted themselves into the corner with no easy way out. But that happened only if the right agency-related questions were asked. Miles usually let them talk their way into it, but then they had to talk their way out of it.

Miles had tried to ask that question in different ways, but it always seemed to come out like that. More than one good listing agent who had sat through a Clear Choice consulting session registered a look of panic when the questions about agency were discussed in plain detail. Sometimes Miles felt the listing agents should struggle with the dilemma, should crack through the ice and fall into the freezing water, should choke on the ethics of the situation. None of them ever said they would compromise their agency to serve two clients. They never would paint the true picture, because they wouldn't want consumers (buyers or sellers) to see it, let alone understand it.

Miles turned west on 86th street and into the sun. The glare made him lower the visor. He lost his thoughts and was paying attention to the traffic. It was only a couple minutes to the cross country course.

The parking lot at Brebeuf, a Jesuit high school in Indianapolis, was full when Miles arrived at the meet. He drove past the light and into a Walmart lot, parked, then walked along a small trail to the back entrance where the race was to be held. His mind was on the cross country meet now. He cut onto the practice course, went down the hill and suddenly was in the midst of prerace activities. The high school tents emblazoned with the colors and names of area schools; the purple of Ben Davis, the gold and black of Warren Central, the green and red of Lawrence North, the yellow and blue of Carmel; then scores of girls all dressed in their school running gear. There were groups of girls jogging in tight groups, crisscrossing the grounds. Miles dodged them with the accuracy of a parent who attended lots of running events.

Miles made his way over to the red and black tent of the North Central Panthers. There were over sixty teammates circulating around the tent. Miles saw his daughter Valerie under the tent huddling with six other girls from the varsity team. The head coach, Jason Nichols, was giving them the final talk before the team went to the starting line.

Miles stood off to the side next to a photographer who was taking a few shots of the huddle.

"Are you with North Central?" Miles asked nicely.

"No, I'm with the Indianapolis Star," the photographer said.

"Oh," said Miles, mildly surprised, "Yeah, North Central is pretty good. I think they're ranked in the top ten."

"They're number four," said the photographer.

The team huddled tightly, then broke and Miles made his way to Valerie. She was barely five feet and 100 pounds. Her blonde hair was pulled back in a knot, and she had a sweatband across her forehead that had 'NCXC' stitched on it. A number was pinned to her uniform.

"Hi, Dad!" Valerie yelled as she ran quickly over to see her father. They embraced.

"Good luck today, honey. Run smart," Miles said. In fact, that's what he said most of the time.

"You know I will,"Valerie said and she kissed him on the cheek and joined the other six runners. The rest of the team gathered around them to whoop it up before the varsity team went to the starting line.

Miles walked over to a group of school parents. They all had on North Central school colors, rooting for their team. They were a group of dedicated parents, ones who brought refreshments to meets, held team meals at home and brought herds of relatives along to cheer the team on. Miles recognized many of the parents and they all waved and said hello.

The best runner on the team was Ellie Master. She would eventually earn a scholarship to a Division 1 school. Miles knew her parents. They were standing next to him in the group. Greg Master was an attorney and his wife, Kyra, was a fitness trainer. They were enthusiastic supporters of the team, as well as conditioned runners.

"Good luck to Ellie today, Greg," Miles said to Mr. Master.

"Oh, hey, thanks, Miles," Greg responded. "Good luck to Valerie, her times are getting faster each week," Greg said.

"She's working hard at it," Miles responded.

Then the gun went off and the crowd cheered. In groups of seven, the line surged forward and they were off. Everybody was yelling.

After the first turn, people started moving to go to different parts of the course to get the next view. Miles stood where he was and noticed a woman, some ten years younger, having a problem with a camera. She was wearing a North Central sweatshirt.

"Can I help you with that?" asked Miles.

"Oh, it's no problem," the woman responded.

Miles saw the problem – it was a safety switch on the camera, the same model that his wife had, with the same problem.

He reached over and clicked the switch. "There, see if it works now," Miles said.

The woman clicked a button and then held the camera up to her face. "It's working now!" she said happily. "Thanks for your help... I'm sorry, I didn't get your name," she said.

"I'm Miles Vincent," he said as he reached out to shake the hand not holding the camera.

"Thank you, Miles. I'm Rhea Master," she stated.

"Are you related to Ellie?" Miles asked.

"I'm her aunt," Rhea said.

"You must know my daughter, Valerie," Miles stated.

"Oh, you're Valerie's dad!" Rhea exclaimed, "she's been over to our house many times," she said it like they were long lost friends.

"I didn't know you were related to Ellie," Miles said. "You're not the same person who works for the Indiana Realtors Association?"

Rhea smiled and said, "I am the legal counsel for the IRA, you know, the voice behind the legal hotline," she said in a self-deprecating tone. It was true. Rhea had gotten her law degree from Indiana University Law School and ended up working at the IRA. The IRA had a legal hotline that allowed principal or managing brokers to call for free legal advice that dealt with real estate. Part of Rhea's job was to manage the service of the legal hotline. The IRA was primarily a lobbying group for realtors and they worked at the state level, addressing laws that affected the real estate industry, rewriting laws, and editing legal documents that licensed real estate agents used in the field.

Then Miles suddenly realized that he had spoken with this woman before! Yes, it had been the very voice on the end of the hotline. And how ironic that they befriend one another at a cross country meet, that they root for the same team, that they work in the same industry!

Rhea didn't know Miles from thousands of other agents who do business in central Indiana. As far as she was concerned, he was just another agent, but having both girls on the team was a real human connection.

Miles spoke to Rhea, "So do you like your job, Rhea?" She was thin, with a hooked nose but was cute.

"Oh, sure, it has its challenges," Rhea said.

"There's certainly room for improvement in our business," Miles said.

"It's been interesting work at this level," Rhea said.

"What do you think about limited agency in Indiana?" Miles asked.

"It's legal, but I wouldn't do it," Rhea said.

"Why not?" Miles asked.

"Because who would want one agent representing the buyer and the seller? The agent is compromised in his ability to represent either client. Any smart person would avoid that."

"But it goes on all the time," Miles said.

"Oh probably not that much," Rhea stated.

"It goes on more than you think," Miles stated, since he knew for sure the local numbers and could see statistically which agents performed limited agency and how often.

Rhea looked at Miles and sized him up. Then she made the connection. This was the guy she had spoken about with Dottie Fuller, the Professional Standards Director at the Indianapolis Board of Realtors. Her stomach tightened a little. He was the one stirring the local waters!

"Rhea, do you think it is fair to home purchasers in Indiana when one agent represents both the buyer and seller in the same transaction? Do you think the potential conflict of interest is enough to warrant some discussion at any level?" Miles asked bluntly.

Rhea's demeanor changed noticeably. She shifted away slightly, like a ship turning broadside to unleash its cannons.

"As long as the proper documents are disclosed and signed by the buyer and seller, it is permissible for the agent to engage in limited agency," Rhea said in canned form. "And as far as any ethical matters, you should probably run that through Indianapolis Board of Realtors. The Professional Standards is the office that deals with business ethics." Rhea almost mentioned that Miles contact Dottie Fuller, but then she decided against it.

Miles looked at Rhea. He could see her running the colors up the flagpole. The bugle had sounded and now she rallied the troops. She was looking at Miles as though he flew the Jolly Roger.

The throng of runners approached. The crowd screamed as the pack of harriers sprinted by. When Miles turned to say something, Rhea was gone.

Bleak Forecast

January 8, 2009

The United States was going to get a new president and Barack Obama would inherit a cesspool of a financial mess in America. The Republicans had bungled too much of the Bush-affected economy, then launched a three-ring circus of a campaign, featuring a trail-blazing soccer mom from Alaska masquerading as a VP on the national ticket – you betcha! There would be no way that the unified Democrats could lose. And they didn't.

The Dow Jones would continue to drop, even as the new president took office. But the damage had been done and no one had a crystal ball to see "Stimulus Package" written on the horizon in green ink, but that is what it would take to pull the country out of one of the biggest economic messes in history, rooted in American greed.

By late 2008, early 2009, the property investors in the US began to see their properties devalued – and that included both owner-occupied homes plus investment property owners. The vast numbers of poor souls that overpaid for homes was too staggering for description. They started dying like flies, flies that couldn't pay the mortgage! Hundreds, then thousands started walking away from their bad investment, leaving the mortgage hanging in the air and welcoming foreclosure. When those thousands walked away from their mortgage obligations, the derivative market began to disintegrate; a sad, devastating effect on all.

The middle class back in America didn't fare as well. Nearly half of the market's value had been wiped out during the market free fall. That meant many of the boomers who were planning to retire suddenly found themselves back at work, postponing the grand retirement vacation because their portfolio was worth half of what it was after the steady decline that didn't end until the Dow Jones sank to 6000 in April of 2009. (Dow Jones is a cousin to Davey Jones, who has a locker near that 6000 number.)

The writing on the wall was legible, and everyone knew who did it. In non-governmental fashion, Washington came down hard and fast on the finance and banking industry. New sanctions would shake down everyone in that business. In Indiana, more than half the mortgage brokers lost their licenses because they couldn't pass the new mandatory test required by the state. On the back side, consumers were seeing the lowest interest rates in decades, but the restrictions to get that money were so tight, only the very credit-worthy could expect to get those rates, and even those credit-worthy folks were getting scrutinized to the nth degree by freaked-out underwriters made nervous by Uncle Sam watching every move. Uncle Sam is still watching them.

Real estate had become a lukewarm enterprise. There were massive numbers of vacant homes all over America. Not the most attractive places to sell. Hundreds of thousands of properties were in the process of foreclosure and in about the same lousy condition as the mortgage-backed securities that backed them, wracking those investors who bought them with staggering losses.

Real estate companies survived, but it was like a plague: large and small agencies alike lost agents to the ravages of the market. The Indianapolis Board of Realtors lost nearly forty percent of its membership due to agents leaving to find some other line of work. It was the lack of business that forced many agents to seek employment elsewhere. But the government sanctions pointed no fingers at how real estate was transacted. It stopped short of finger pointing maybe because the Feds thought they got the bad guys already. The realtors didn't change the way they were doing business, they just didn't have any.

So maybe the timing would be right to introduce a new order, a new ethical improvement about the way residential homes are bought and sold. That's what Miles was thinking.

But even in times like these, the local and state real estate officials maintained their cozy jobs as they observed the real estate carnage from inside their protected cubicles. Sonny Scheizer, Dottie Fuller, and Rhea Master all had their jobs, they didn't feel the plunging market, their paychecks weren't dependent on a commission, they didn't despair like the rest of the agents did. Getting paid a salary in a real estate was like working in the mail room during the Vietnam War stateside: not much chance of being hit by shrapnel.

Easy money had become a victim.

Bleaker Forecast

By 2009, the real estate market was doing pretty well in some areas, in other areas not so well. The Federal Government had extended the buyer tax credit program which helped to stimulate some home purchases. It helped as savvy buyers scrambled on deals prior to the deadline. The property meltdown affected some neighborhoods drastically; if there were a large percentage of foreclosures in a particular neighborhood, the chance that values would drop was almost certain. For neighborhoods where few foreclosures occurred, the chance to experience property devaluation was lessened. This was the best situation property owners could hope for: homes retaining value when there were few or no foreclosures available for comparison.

When multiple foreclosures occurred, the downturn in property values, in that area, was scary. The vast amount of foreclosure property clogged up the market, and when they mixed in with other sales, especially from an appraisal perspective, it further declined the value of property, especially property that was in or near the area of foreclosure. No wonder the Federal Government told the big three banks in November of 2010 to hold off on declaring more foreclosures; the devaluing aspect of these properties had meant that regular folks couldn't even refinance because now their homes were worth less than they were ten years ago!

This general devaluation also killed a lot of deals. Transactions fell apart because appraisers were strict on the comparable homes they were permitted to use to determine value: any sale over six months was considered to be toxic inventory and it was not to be used in the valuation of a current sale. If an agent couldn't use a good home sale comparable that was older than six months, then it might limit the upward value sellers are hoping for. The tide was turning in a bad way.

The crimping of home values became shocking for the seller and the buyer alike. Now the transaction was back on the table to renegotiate the sale price. Why? Because loans are based off the appraised value, not what a buyer agrees to pay on the purchase agreement. Would the seller be willing to bite that bullet to renegotiate a lower price, or should they refuse the deal and wait the bear property market out?

For some savvy buyers, it also worked the other way: in some areas, desperate sellers were taking much less than their houses were worth. It could be a buyers market for years, so savvy buyers' agents could throw out low-ball offers from well-qualified individuals and often score a great deal. But in general the market became flat, like the Gulf on a windless morning. Despite the economic disaster brought on by the greed of Wall Street, the real estate industry didn't change much.

Miles had concluded that the real estate industry worked hard to maintain its old ways and was reluctant to change. He had spoken to many people who worked in the business and although they agreed with the concept, they all quietly agreed to be quiet. The reality of Miles' idea was that nobody wanted to talk about it. They didn't want to stir the waters of real estate representation.

The 30 Second Rule, Again

May 20, 2011

Miles was late for a late afternoon lunch with his pals and cohorts, Vance Ingalls and Jake Brandon. Miles looked at his phone knowing he was a few minutes late. He hated to be late.

The express elevator was zipping Miles up to the top floor of the Skyline Club. He swallowed to lessen the pressure in his ears and looked up to see what floor he was on. The elevator made a ding and came to a stop.

Miles walked quickly into the club and over to the bar area which looked southeast over the city. He entered the dining room and saw his good friends sitting by the window.

As Miles approached, they both looked at their wristwatches.

"Hey Vance, hey Jake," Miles said. "Sorry I'm late." Miles saw them looking at their watches and was apologetic in his tone.

Both men laughed as Miles sat down. "We're just kidding you," Jake replied. "You're only a few minutes late."

"Well, you know I don't like to be late," Miles said.

"Loosen up, Miles," Vance said. "We haven't even ordered."

Miles sat down and took a drink of the ice water.

"How's the consulting work coming along, Miles?" Vance asked.

"Pretty good, I guess," Miles said. "I haven't been making any headway with the real estate industry, but sellers really like it. Most of my consulting business has come from sellers who use the service, then tell someone else about it."

Miles suddenly perked up for no apparent reason.

"Vance, you remember what you said to me last time we met?" Miles asked.

Vance sat back in his chair with a blank look. He couldn't recall what he had said to Miles.

"You don't remember, do you?" Miles asked pointedly. "I'll give you a hint: thirty seconds."

"Oh yeah, now I remember," Vance said immediately. "I had commented about your idea, that you only had thirty seconds to explain the concept to a consumer or it would not work."

"That's right!" Miles said loudly. Loud enough that the people sitting at the table next to them looked at Miles, wondering what made him yell.

"Vance, I think you're right. I have thought a lot about this since you mentioned it that last time we met. So now I have a little surprise for you," Miles said.

And then he stood up at the table, as though he were looking at two brand new clients.

"Time me on this, will you Vance?" Miles asked. This is the concept whittled down to a thirty seconds."

"The Clear Choice consulting method is a new concept for sellers who want to hire the best real estate agent at the best price. We provide sellers with pertinent sales statistics of agents who have specifically sold homes in their area. The seller selects three agents from the group, we contact the agents and arrange for three separate listing presentations with the agents who are chosen. We attend the presentations with the seller, help them understand the process, and help negotiate the best possible listing contract for the seller," Miles said. "Whew, did I make it in thirty seconds?" Miles asked.

"Thirty-two seconds," Vance replied.

"Shit. There's still another part I have to explain," Miles said.

"What's that?" asked Jake.

"The part about buyers," Miles said.

"What about the buyers?" Jake asked.

"Well, the nice part about the consulting service is that it sets up buyers beautifully," Miles said. "When we work with a buyer, we can promise them that we will never compromise our ability to represent them, because we don't list properties."

"That sounds like another thirty seconds of explaining," Vance replied.

"C'mon, Vance, give me a break!" Miles complained.

"Just being honest with you, Miles," said Vance.

"And I was all excited that I had whittled the explaining down to thirty seconds!" Miles whined. "You popped my bubble, Vance."

"Like I said before, if you can't do it in thirty seconds, then maybe you ought to write a book instead," Vance remarked, half joking.

Miles sat down and spoke to Vance. "That's not a bad idea."

The Fishy Side of Real Estate

EPILOGUE

May 18, 2015

The gull shrieked as Miles readied the boat for departure. He looked up as the birds flew by, complaining. Miles had nothing to complain about as his life was more about fishing than selling real estate. He didn't have to work as much anymore. His boat, a 44-foot Hatteras aptly named 'Clear Choice', was only one year old and it had all the latest upgrades and gadgetry. Last year, Miles had bought a small condo in Port Aransas and had rented a boat slip in the Port Aransas City Harbor. The morning was still and the temperature was already in the eighties. Miles was excited to take his guests along, who were visiting from Indiana.

The sun was up, but it was still before 7 am. Even though he had two deckhands helping to prepare the boat for the fishing trip, Miles still enjoyed the routine of getting everything into tiptop shape.

As he was loading ice into a cooler he heard the creaking of the wooden dock as four people made their way to the boat. He walked to the stern of the boat and met the group as they arrived.

"My man, Mitch!" Miles yelled, in a teasing manner. He was addressing the former Governor of Indiana, Mitch Daniels. He had brought his wife Cheri along with another couple from Indiana. Miles had invited the former Governor and his wife earlier in the year. Mitch had retired from politics and had more leisure time to do things now that he was out of office. They had flown directly to the small Port Aransas airport on a private plane.

Miles greeted each one as they walked up the gangway.

"Looks like we can be out of here in about ten minutes," Miles said. He glanced up to the bridge where one of the deckhands was working. "Hey Pete, think we're about ready?" he asked.

"I'm about done up here, Mr. Vincent. I need just a few more minutes," Pete said.

Mitch spoke to Miles, "Cheri and I have been looking forward to this trip for months, Miles. We're excited to spend the day fishing on the Gulf of Mexico," he said.

The former Governor liked Miles, even though what he had done had caused a major upheaval in the residential real estate business. It was an unlikely approach that Miles had used, but that approach had turned the residential real estate industry upside down and eventually, the law changed, at least in Indiana.

It wasn't so much the business of Clear Choice Realtors and the innovative concept that Miles had created several years ago – it was the book, *The Fishy Side of Real Estate*. It was just a short novel about real estate with an odd fishing metaphor, but it had gone viral. Initially, the self-published book sales started slowly, in fact, Miles only had 200 copies printed. But it didn't take long for the word to get out once it hit Facebook, Twitter and various real estate blog sites. Within months sales improved to the point that Miles negotiated to have the book reprinted by a large publisher. Then the word really got out.

Although the real estate industry wasn't thrilled with the book, it was the home buying and selling public that seemed to appreciate it. Once the book sold 100,000 copies (mostly in Indiana) the effect was stunning.

Even though it was a novel, consumers who read the book understood the importance of real estate agency. For them, it was like putting on a mask and snorkel while swimming the Great Barrier Reef of real estate – suddenly, many things became clear.

Weeks after the book became public, the calls and e-mails started coming in. At first, it was just a few people who contacted the Attorney General's Office. But within the year the complaints were daily. Miles' book had put a spotlight on the issue and now consumers understood with uncommon alacrity, the disadvantages of dual representation.

Enough complaints were filed and enough politicians were contacted that it became a statewide issue. Not even the powerful real estate lobbies could stop the change. And what a change it was: the State of Indiana eventually passed a law that made it illegal for one agent to represent a buyer and seller in the same residential sales transaction.

"Is anyone prone to seasickness?" Miles asked. "Once we get out beyond land sight, you might get a little queasy, unless you're used to it," Miles stated. "We have patches that will keep you from getting seasick, just in case it gets a little rough."

The former Governor slapped Miles on the back and replied, "Miles, if I knew what I know now, I would have asked for that patch a couple years ago!"

Everyone on the boat laughed, because they could laugh about it now.

A new methodology, an idea born out of logic and fairness to home buyers and sellers: Miles' novel concept had shrugged the atlas of residential real estate.

Pete yelled from the bridge, "We're ready to shove off!"